JUMP BALL

Also by Adrienne Mercer
in the Lorimer Sports Stories series

Rebound

JUMP BALL

Adrienne Mercer

James Lorimer & Company Ltd., Publishers
Toronto

James Lorimer & Company Ltd., Publishers acknowledges the support of the Ontario Arts Council. We acknowledge the financial support of the Government of Canada through the Canada Book Fund for our publishing activities. We acknowledge the support of the Canada Council for the Arts which last year invested $24.3 million in writing and publishing throughout Canada. We acknowledge the Government of Ontario through the Ontario Media Development Corporation's Ontario Book Initiative.

Cover Image: Shutterstock

Library and Archives Canada Cataloguing in Publication

Mercer, Adrienne
    Jump ball / Adrienne Mercer.

(Sports stories)
Issued also in an electronic format.
ISBN 978-1-4594-0180-8 (bound).--ISBN 978-1-4594-0179-2 (pbk.)

    I. Title. II. Series: Sports stories (Toronto, Ont.)

PS8576.E64J86 2012   jC813'.6   C2012-903692-7

James Lorimer & Company Ltd., Publishers	Distributed in the United States by: Orca Book Publishers
317 Adelaide Street West, Suite 1002	P.O. Box 468
Toronto, ON, Canada	Custer, WA USA
M5V 1P9	98240-0468
www.lorimer.ca	

Printed and bound in Canada.
Manufactured by Friesens Corporation in Altona, Manitoba, Canada in August 2012.
Job #77079

To Mom, Dad, Jason, Carol, Holden,
John, Barbara, and Greg,
and of course,
to Michael, Lucas, and Emily

CONTENTS

1 THE END OF SUMMER

Abby dribbled the ball toward the net as her sister Sarah closed in quickly on her right side. Another few steps and Abby knew she'd have a basket. Sarah was all over the place though, a determined flurry of arms and legs. No matter how hard Abby tried to avoid Sarah, her sister kept blocking her. Frustrated, Abby backed off — instead of the layup she'd been planning, she attempted a shot from halfway down the driveway. It bounced off the rim and Sarah lunged for it. The two girls moved across their makeshift court, their long dark hair swishing as they tried to fake each other out. Abby was slightly taller, and Sarah's hair was wavy while her sister's was straight. Overall, though, they looked enough alike that they could easily have been twins.

"You still can't beat me at the long shots!" Sarah crowed. She darted away from Abby and then circled back toward the basketball hoop, pivoting to position her body between Abby and the ball. Abby intercepted and set herself up to shoot.

"Aw, come on, Abby. That should have been mine!" Sarah complained.

"I can't help it if I'm quicker than you are!" Abby teased. She swiveled away from Sarah and sent the ball swooshing through the basket. As Sarah sprung up for the ball, Abby sprawled out on the cool concrete and chugged from her water bottle.

"I'll beat you next time," Sarah vowed. Her voice was good-natured as she looked down at her older sister. She made a perfect three-point shot, flopped down next to Abby, and began bouncing the ball against the wall of their father's detached workshop. Bounce. Catch. Bounce. Catch. Bounce.

Abby eased back until she was flat against the pavement gazing up at the summer sky. It was seven o'clock on a sunny August night, one week before the start of the new school year. Abby wished her evenings could go on like this forever — barbecue dinners with her family, goofing off afterward with the basketball or just lounging in the yard talking with her sister. Instead, it was already time to go back to Harewood Secondary.

Abby and Sarah had lived in the same house since they were born, in a quiet area near downtown Nanaimo. Abby was about to start grade nine at Harewood, while Sarah would be starting grade eight — her first year at the high school — in just a few days.

"Are you nervous about school?" Abby asked her sister. She remembered her first day at Harewood. The school had seemed huge, and she'd felt out of place among so many unfamiliar faces. *I still feel like that a lot of the time*, she realized.

"Not really," Sarah replied, continuing to bounce and catch the ball as she spoke. "I'll probably recognize a few people from elementary school. A lot of kids are going to other schools, but I'm sure I won't be the only one going to Harewood." Bounce. Catch. "Besides, you'll be there!"

"Yeah, but *I* don't know anyone there very well . . . just Lisa, really." Lisa Cairns, Abby's closest friend, was the daughter of Abby and Sarah's mother's closest friend.

Abby sighed. "I guess I still like books more than I like people. I haven't made many new friends at Harewood." She sat up and stretched out her legs.

"At least you get good grades," Sarah reassured her. "I wish I was better at that part of school! Are classes a lot harder in grade eight?"

Abby shrugged. "Not really. You just have to do the work, just like in elementary school."

Sarah snorted. "Like I said, I wish I was better at that stuff. I'm sure I'll get by." She paused, and then asked, "Are there lots of clubs and stuff at Harewood? Do they organize intramural sports or anything?"

"I never asked about that. You'll have to find out on the first day. I'm pretty sure they have all the usual teams though. Basketball, football, field hockey, all that kind of stuff."

Sarah bounced the ball against the workshop wall once more. "Abby, we should join the junior girls' basketball team! My old gym teacher suggested it to me. It's for grade eight and nine girls, so we could do it together. It would be so much fun and we'd meet lots of people that way!"

"Yeah, right," Abby answered. "That's not going to happen." Secretly she liked the idea of being on a team, but not necessarily with Sarah. She didn't like the idea of her younger, more outgoing sister outshining her at school.

Sarah pushed her dark brown, wavy hair off her face and, in a few quick motions, slipped an elastic band from her wrist and fastened her ponytail. "Why not? We shoot hoops together all the time."

"I know, but we're only playing for fun. We goof around and shove each other, and it never matters if we finish a game or not. Playing for the Harewood Hawks would be different. I'm not really into the whole team thing."

"Oh, come on, Abby! You can handle it! It wouldn't kill you to be a little more social. Don't you think it would be fun? We could have lots of the same friends." Sarah smiled. "Remember when we played lunchtime basketball two years ago? I loved that. Everybody joined!"

"I only did that for a few weeks, remember? I dropped out to be a reading buddy for the little kids," said Abby.

"Oh, that's right," Sarah replied. "What was it you said? *Reading is cooler than running around and sweating*?"

"Something like that." Abby smiled.

"Well, I still thought it was fun playing basketball with you," Sarah said. She thunked the ball against the workshop wall again, and then clapped her hand across her mouth as the door creaked open.

"Dad, I'm sorry!" Sarah exclaimed. "I didn't know you were still working in there."

The girls' father grinned at them. His work shorts and T-shirt were splattered with black paint and his sandy hair was sweaty and even wavier than usual. His job was making props for TV, movies, and theatre companies. He spent most days in the shop, building his creations.

"I thought I'd better get out of there before the whole wall came down," he teased. "Lucky I wasn't painting anything too delicate, Sarah." He sat down between Sarah and Abby. "What are you two up to besides trashing my shop?"

"I'm trying to convince Abby to try out for the Junior Hawks basketball team with me," Sarah blurted out.

"And I'm trying to explain to her that it's a terrible idea," Abby countered. "It's not my kind of thing."

"I think you're scared," Sarah said. "That's totally why you're saying no. You're scared that you won't make the team."

"I am not."

Sarah made a face at her. "Well, if you're not up for it, I guess I'll just try out on my own and amaze everyone with my awesome skills."

Abby snorted. "Yeah, right." She reached for the basketball and gave it a solid thunk against the workshop wall, ignoring her sister's amused look.

"You might just surprise yourself and have fun," their dad said, smiling at Abby. "I played basketball in high school and I had a great time."

I don't want Sarah to think I'm scared to join the team, Abby thought. *I'm her older sister — if she can do it, I can do it. Besides, maybe Dad is right.*

"Okay, I'll try out," she told Sarah. "Why not?"

2 FIRST DAY

A week later, Abby and Lisa stood outside Sarah's last class — history — waiting for her to emerge. Usually Abby felt frustrated when Sarah dawdled, but she couldn't help grinning as she watched her sister talking excitedly to another girl. *She's already a part of things*, Abby thought jealously.

"Looks like Sarah's already feeling at home," she told Lisa.

"When has Sarah ever *not* felt at home?" Lisa asked. "She's spent her whole life being outgoing."

That's true, Abby thought. *Sarah just barges in and makes friends everywhere she goes. Lisa and I tend to watch and wait.*

"Do you ever wish we were more like she is?" Abby asked Lisa. "Anyone looking at us right now would think *we* were the new kids at Harewood."

"I do sometimes wish I was as outgoing as Sarah," Lisa admitted, fiddling with one of her lightning-bolt earrings. "The thing is, being shy has been good for me. If I wasn't shy, I probably wouldn't have got so into playing guitar and writing music. I'm not a really outgoing person, but I'm okay with that."

Abby nodded. "So . . . there's no chance you're going to try out for the Hawks with us?"

Lisa laughed. "Why would I do that? I'd never have any time to play guitar! Don't get any ideas, Abby. I'm just coming along today for support."

"All right, I'll stop asking," Abby said good-naturedly. She caught her sister's eye and motioned for her to hurry up. Sarah quickly said goodbye to the girl she'd been talking with and bustled out into the hall.

"Sorry, you guys," she said. "I was just talking with Katelyn . . . she was in my class last year."

"Right, I remember you talking about her," said Abby. "Sorry to make you rush but it's almost time for tryouts."

"Thanks," said Sarah. "I feel a bit scattered today. There's so much going on! I sort of had this impression about high school . . . I probably got it from TV," she said. "I didn't expect the kids to be so nice. I met this girl in my art class, Ella. She's so much fun. And this other girl from art, Jessie, said she's trying out for the Junior Hawks too." She took a breath, finally, and smiled at Abby. "I really like this school."

"I'm glad," Abby said. She felt pleased for her sister, but envious too. After a whole year at Harewood, Abby still felt like a loner. "You meet people so quickly. It's like you barely even have to try."

"It's probably because I was just so excited about high school," Sarah said. "I'm excited about tryouts too. If we make the team, we are going to have so much fun."

"I think you'll both make it, no problem," Lisa said.

3 TRYOUTS

In the gym, they joined the thirty or so other girls sitting on the bleachers. Sarah waved enthusiastically at a girl with curly blond hair who was sitting in the bottom row.

"Hi, Jessie!" she said. "This is my sister, Abby, and our friend, Lisa."

"Hi!" said Jessie. She patted the bench next to her and the three of them sat down. "Are you all trying out, or just Sarah?"

"Abby and I are," said Sarah. "Lisa came to watch."

"I've never tried out for anything like this before," said Jessie nervously.

"Neither have we," Sarah reassured her. "We played basketball in elementary school, but just for fun. Everyone got to be on the team."

Abby scanned the bleachers and noticed that quite a few of the girls had been in her classes the previous year. She couldn't remember ever having a real conversation with any of them. *I bet none of those girls remember me*, she thought.

"Who's the coach?" Sarah asked.

Abby pointed toward the gym doors, one of which had just opened. "Looks like it's Ms. Marshall," said Abby. "The vice-principal."

"Was she the coach last year too?" Sarah asked. Abby shrugged.

"I don't think so," Lisa answered. "I think last year's coach only did it for one year. There was another coach who was here for years and years, but she retired. When she left, the team lost the district championships for the first time in ages."

"How do you know that?" Abby asked with surprise.

"I saw it in the newspaper last year."

"*You* look at the sports section of the newspaper?" Sarah asked, laughing. "I thought sports weren't your thing."

Lisa smiled. "My mom took photos at the tournament and some of them were used in the story." Lisa's mother was a photographer, and she often did work for the school district.

"What's Ms. Marshall like?" Sarah asked.

"I don't know. She only teaches grade twelve classes," Abby said.

"I don't know anything about her either," Lisa said.

"I guess you two never get sent to the vice-principal's office for bad behaviour?" asked Sarah with a sly grin.

Abby scoffed and kicked her sister lightly in the

shin as Ms. Marshall walked to the centre of the gym. She was exceptionally tall, and somehow her short red hair made her seem even taller.

"Hi everyone, I'm Coach Marshall," she said in a clear, strong voice. "Thank you all for coming to the Junior Hawks tryouts. If I had my way, I would include each and every one of you on the team. Our budget is limited and so is our practice time, so our team can only have twenty girls. That said, if you try out this year and you don't make it, don't let that discourage you. Both the Junior Hawks and the Senior Hawks look for new players every year. Okay?" The girls all nodded.

"This is my first year as coach and I'm looking forward to the challenge," Coach Marshall continued. "Here's what I'm looking for today."

As Coach Marshall droned on about teamwork, fun, community involvement, and school spirit, Abby began to daydream about being the best player on the Junior Hawks. She'd be the fastest runner, the best dribbler, the most accurate shooter — and she'd be the most popular player on the team, even more popular than Sarah. At the end of the season, everyone would vote for Abby as the most valuable player!

Abby's daydreaming came to an abrupt end when Lisa elbowed her in the ribs. "What are you thanking me for?" Lisa asked.

"Huh?"

"You were muttering 'thank you, thank you,'" Lisa

whispered, her expression amused. "Are you paying attention?"

"Of course," Abby whispered back, and stared straight ahead, embarrassed, hoping that she looked as attentive as the other girls did. Lisa rolled her eyes, but she didn't say anything else.

"Motivation is extremely important, and so is your willingness to work with your teammates," Coach Marshall was saying. She paused, staring hard at each girl in turn. "As you know, Harewood Secondary was district champion for nine years, until we lost to Nanaimo Secondary last year. It would be a real victory for Harewood athletics to win back that championship, so we will work toward that goal." Her gaze seemed to burn into the eyes of each hopeful athlete.

I know how to be the best student in class, Abby thought. *This doesn't sound much different. I just need to work really hard to be the best player on the Hawks.*

The coach was still studying the group of girls in front of her. "All right," she said finally. "Come on over to the equipment room with me and we'll get some basketballs."

"I like her," Abby whispered to Sarah.

Sarah grinned. "I do too."

They each high-fived Lisa and then followed the rest of the group to the equipment room, where Coach Marshall was tossing a basketball to each girl in turn. When everyone had a ball, the coach took a quick roll call and then asked the players to space themselves out evenly across the gym.

"I'm going to start you out with something simple," she said. "I'd like you all to dribble the ball ten times, pivot five times, and then repeat."

Abby concentrated on her style, trying to make each bounce of the ball the same height, each pivot strong and graceful.

"Good work," Coach Marshall told her as she walked among the hopefuls. Abby beamed. From the bleachers, Lisa smiled her approval and gave her a quick thumbs-up.

After about five minutes, the coach instructed the girls to pair off. Sarah ran straight over to Abby.

"Partners?" she asked.

"Sure."

The coach asked a girl named Emiko to help demonstrate a bounce pass and a chest pass. Emiko had super-short black hair and wore blue nail polish. She reminded Abby of the pictures of musicians she'd seen in Lisa's magazines. Emiko wasn't as tall as some of the other girls, but Abby could tell by the way she moved that she was an experienced basketball player.

"Now it's your turn," the coach told the group. "Work with your partner to get comfortable with these passes."

Abby looked around and realized that some of the girls were just starting to learn how to control the ball. Abby already knew how, after years of playing in elementary school gym class and out in the yard with Sarah.

"Isn't this fun, Abby?" asked Sarah, bounce-passing to her sister.

"It kind of is," Abby agreed, sending a chest pass back to Sarah. Maybe you were right about the whole team thing. I might just start to like it!"

Next, Coach Marshall demonstrated how to do a layup, Abby's specialty. When it was her turn, the ball sailed beautifully into the net.

"That was fabulous, Abby!" Coach exclaimed. Abby beamed.

Sarah was next up and she started off well, but her timing was off. When she went up for her shot, the ball fell uselessly to the ground.

"Nice try, Sarah," Coach said.

Abby smirked. Sarah noticed.

"What are you laughing at?" grumbled Sarah as she took her place in line next to Abby.

"Sorry. That just looked sort of . . . funny. Not exactly graceful."

"Shush," Sarah said, trying to laugh as she swatted Abby's arm.

"Make me." Abby said, giggling.

Abby's turn came around again. She completed a flawless layup and then made a quick chest pass back to Sarah, who fumbled the ball.

"Oops!" Abby said lightly. Sarah glared.

Finally, Coach had everyone line up to take three shots each at the free-throw line. Two of Abby's shots went in, and all three of Sarah's.

"Nice!" Abby cheered. Sarah smiled and took a mock bow.

"Great work, everyone!" Coach said. "Thanks for trying out for the Hawks. I'll post the team roster on my office door tomorrow at noon, and our first practice will be right after school. If you're on the roster, I'll meet you here. If you're not, don't give up — I'll be happy to talk to you about improvements you could make if you'd like to try out again. As I said, I wish I could include each and every one of you on the team."

★★★

Lisa needed to get home right after tryouts, but Sarah wanted to stay behind to chat with Jessie and some of the other girls.

"See you at home." Abby waved to her sister. "I'm going to keep Lisa company."

"Sure, Abby," Sarah said. "Thanks for coming to watch us, Lisa. See you tomorrow."

Abby waved at the other girls, and she and Lisa ducked out the back door of the gym.

"Whew," Abby said, stretching her arms over her head. "I'm tired!"

"I bet," said Lisa. "That was intense for a beginners'

practice! You looked great out there, by the way."

"Thanks. Now I just need to wait and see if the coach thinks so too."

Lisa nodded. "So, what will you do if you make the team and Sarah doesn't?"

Abby snickered. "That's *not* going to happen."

"It might, especially since Sarah's a year younger than you," said Lisa, tucking her chin-length light brown hair behind her ears. "If there are a bunch of people with about the same skills, maybe the coach will choose older girls over younger ones. Or maybe something will make you stand out more than Sarah. It could happen."

"I guess you're right," Abby replied. She liked the idea of beating Sarah at something — earlier, when Sarah had fumbled the ball, Abby was glad to realize that her sister didn't shine at absolutely everything. She imagined her parents and Sarah cheering from the bleachers while she led the team to victory. Fantasizing was a lot different from actually seeing her sister miss out on a spot with the Hawks, though.

"Joining the team was Sarah's idea," Abby reasoned. "The whole point was that we'd get to play basketball together. I'll feel bad if she doesn't make the cut."

"I know," Lisa said. She paused. "So does that mean you'll quit the team if you make it and Sarah doesn't?"

Abby shook her head. "That would be silly," she said firmly. "No way."

4 READY TO PLAY

The next day, Sarah eagerly squeezed her way through the small cluster of girls gathered in front of Coach Marshall's office door, while Abby hung back and waited for her sister to announce the result. Her conversation with Lisa the previous afternoon replayed in her mind as she watched Sarah edge toward the front of the group. Abby kind of liked the thought of being the only sister on the team. At the same time, she didn't want her sister to be upset. It would be better if they both made it.

When Sarah saw the roster, she let out a giant whoop and raced through the crowd to bear-hug Abby.

"We did it!" she shouted.

Abby grinned and hugged her sister back.

"Congratulations, you guys!" Jessie called out as she skipped excitedly toward them. "I'm so glad all three of us made it! Isn't this great?"

"Totally," Sarah said. Sarah chatted away with the others while Abby listened without joining in.

Why can't I ever think of anything to say in situations like this? Abby asked herself. *Sarah can talk to anybody, anytime. I always just stand there. It's like I need an invitation or something!* Frustrated, she vowed that she would work as hard as she could to be the best player on the Harewood Junior Hawks. Then everyone would want to talk with her ... and it might be a little bit easier to come up with something to say.

***

After school Abby met Sarah outside her history class. After a quick stop at their lockers, the two girls headed into the change room.

"Hey, it's the sisters!" A tall pretty girl with long red hair walked over. Her name was Sam — Abby had seen her around school before. "I knew you two would make it," the girl said. "You looked great at tryouts!" She paused. "You're Abby, right?"

"Yeah," said Abby.

"I thought so," Sam said. "Didn't we have math together last year? Or was it history class?"

"Um, math, I think," Abby said.

"Thought so," Sam said, smiling. She picked up her water bottle and with a friendly "See you out there," she pushed through the door into the gym.

"She seems nice," Sarah said. "At tryouts I think she said she was on the team last year too."

"Yeah, I think you're right," Abby said.

"You didn't really know her last year, did you?"

"Nope."

"She seems to like you. Everyone does, Abby. Did you do that thing when you started school here where you don't talk to anyone you don't know?"

"I don't know what you're talking about," Abby answered.

"Sure you do. You do it all the time, for no reason."

Abby sighed. "Well, if I do it all the time, then yes, I guess I probably did it all last year when I was in grade eight here." She glanced at the bench next to Sarah. "Is that *my* green T-shirt?" she asked, happy for a reason to change the subject.

"Maybe," Sarah said with a wicked grin. She pulled the shirt over her head and dashed out into the gym with Abby hot on her heels. Trading mock-angry looks, they joined their teammates at the centre of the court.

"Welcome back," Coach Marshall said with a smile. "You all did a great job at tryouts and I'm proud to have you on the team. I have some ideas about who to pick for team captain, but I won't decide until the end of practice." She wrapped her arms across her chest, stretching the muscles in her back.

"All right, let's start with a passing drill called clap pass — everyone make a circle around me, please."

Abby stood close to Coach Marshall and listened carefully to the rules of the drill. Coach was going to pass the ball to random players, and the girls needed to clap before catching the ball.

"You're out if you don't clap, if you miss the ball, or if you clap when I fake a pass," Coach said. "Here we go."

The first pass went to Jessie, who easily clapped and caught it. Next came a faked pass to a player named Kim — who figured out the trick — and a neat chest pass to Sarah, who also managed to clap.

When Abby's first pass came, it was easier to clap and catch than she'd anticipated. As girls began dropping out, though, the passes sped up and the fakes got harder to identify. Sarah missed a clap and had to join the others on the sidelines. It was down to Abby, Emiko, and Sam. After what seemed like forever, Emiko got fooled by a faked pass and Abby missed the ball while trying to clap.

"Sam wins!" Coach Marshall exclaimed and the girls all applauded and cheered. Abby scuffed a foot along the floor of the gym, frustrated. In her classes, she found it so easy to get all the right answers and score the highest marks. Basketball was going to be a little bit tougher.

"Now it's time for a partner passing drill," announced the coach. "Everyone choose a partner, grab a ball, and work on all of your passes. I'm looking for bounce passes, chest passes, overhead, and baseball style. Go for it!"

Sarah grabbed Abby's arm and together they ran to the bin of balls.

"Let's do overhead first," Sarah suggested. Abby backed up to give Sarah some room. She caught Sarah's pass easily and returned one of her own. Sarah bounce-passed back and Abby returned the ball the same way. A ball bounced through their play area and Kim scurried through to retrieve it.

"Sorry," she called out.

Sarah grinned and shot a fast chest pass to Abby. "Good thing you got out of the way in time," she joked to Kim.

They switched to baseball-type passes, then started mixing things up — Sarah bounced the ball to Abby, Abby returned a chest pass, and Sarah tried an overhead. Soon their time was up and Coach gave three sharp blasts on the whistle.

"Okay, that was great. All of you chose the same partner you worked with last time, though," she said. "I was going to set up a scrimmage for the last half of practice, but instead I'd like to see you do that drill again with a different partner. Afterwards you can stick with that partner for some one-on-one."

Coach paired Abby with Sam, and Sarah with Emiko, and they started the passing drill again.

"Ready?" Sam asked. She chest-passed the ball to Abby, and Abby caught it neatly and returned a bounce pass.

"Hey, I think you've done this before," Sam joked kindly as she returned the pass. Abby smiled slightly and kept focused on the drill. She had expected the drill to be harder against a more experienced partner, but anticipating Sam's movements was easier than she'd thought.

"Wow," Sam said after a few more passes. "Even when I try to fake you out, you know what to do. Are you sure you weren't on the Hawks last year?" she teased.

"I just play at home for fun. Sarah and I have a hoop," Abby said.

"Cool!" Sam replied.

Abby wished conversation came easily to her. She couldn't think of anything else to say to Sam so she just stopped talking.

"Let's switch to one-on-one," Sam said. "I'll start and you try to steal the ball." Sam had barely started to dribble when Abby found an opening and got possession of the ball.

"That was great," Sam said. "Okay, now I'll try to steal it from you." Abby tried her hardest to keep away from Sam, pivoting and making sure her body was always between Sam and the ball. Eventually she slipped up and skipped a dribble, and Sam moved in neatly to take the ball over.

"Great job," Sam said again.

Abby smiled a thin smile as she reviewed the play in

her mind, figuring out where she'd gone wrong.

"Let's try again," Abby suggested, but practice was over and Coach Marshall blew her whistle to call everyone back to the centre of the gym.

"I'm impressed by your hard work today," she said. "Your skills are already improving — and that is exactly what we need so we can win back the district championship." She glanced at her notes and then looked up at the group. "I've chosen co-captains for the team this year instead of just one captain. Congratulations, Emiko and Sam!"

"They'll be perfect. I like the way they play," Sarah said to Abby. "Emiko was a real challenge for me just now. She is such a good player that I had trouble keeping up. I guess you had the same experience with Sam?"

"Not really," said Abby. "I guess she and Emiko have more experience than we do, though." She headed to the change room, wondering if Sam would have been named co-captain if Abby hadn't let her steal the ball.

5 SISTER SITUATION

With her backpack half-hanging off her right shoulder, Abby raced toward the change room a few days later, eager to play her first home game.

"Hey, Abby, how's it going?" asked Emiko, who was already changed and doing her pre-practice stretches.

"Not bad, thanks," Abby replied. She pulled her casual purple top up over her head, quickly replacing it with an old grey T-shirt.

"How about you?" she asked Emiko awkwardly.

"I'm doing great. I can't wait until we get our new uniforms," Emiko said excitedly.

"Oh I know! Those old ones looked so worn out ... and they've been out of style for years. I am so glad we don't have to use them again," Sam chimed in from the other end of the room.

"When do we get them?" Abby asked.

"Coach is going to let us know today. The colours are the same as always, blue and gold, but we chose new lettering and new styles and stuff at the end of last year.

Too bad you didn't get to help, but I think you'll like what we picked." Emiko looked at her watch. "Almost time to get out there. Hey, Abby, where's your sister?"

"I'm here!" Sarah burst through the change-room door and collapsed onto one of the narrow benches that ran the length of the room. "We were watching a film in class and it ran overtime." Hurriedly she dumped her basketball gear out onto the bench beside her and began to swap school clothes for gym clothes.

"Your shorts are on backwards," Abby told Sarah with a grin.

Sarah tossed a balled-up sock in her sister's direction, and Abby batted it away, laughing. "At least I told you before you got onto the court!"

"I guess that's true," said Sarah as she jammed her overflowing backpack into a locker. "What would I do without you, Abby?" She sighed dramatically and Abby laughed.

The two girls followed Emiko onto the court, where Coach Marshall stood waiting beside an enormous rectangular box.

"Your uniforms arrived," she sang out, and the team flocked around her, eager for a first glimpse.

"I love them," Sam exclaimed, and the other girls echoed her excitement, reaching to touch the shiny blue fabric, gold lettering, and hawk outline.

"Not so fast, not so fast!" Coach Marshall laughed. "Wait until I call your name. These are arranged by size and I don't want to have to re-sort everything. Oh, and by the way, we will have to do some fundraising to pay the school back for these. We'll get started once you've had the chance to work together as a team for a few practices and games." With that, she began to call out names. As each girl replied, Coach tossed her a uniform. Before long everyone was modelling the sleeveless shirts and long, loose shorts.

Abby ran her hand up and down her belly, enjoying the feel of the shiny material. "We look like a professional team!" she exclaimed.

"You do look great — all of you," Coach agreed. "Now remember . . . what Harewood needs is a team that looks great *and* plays great. We want to win this district. Remember that every time you put your uniforms on, you have a job to do. I'll be watching."

"Whoa, she's *intense*," Sarah muttered.

Abby gave her sister a surprised look.

"What's *your* problem? Don't you want to win?" Abby asked.

"Well, yeah . . . but let's get realistic. We're a bunch of thirteen- and fourteen-year-olds!"

Abby shook her head at Sarah. "What? We're a serious team! Don't you think so?"

"Abby, Sarah, what are you whispering about?" Coach Marshall asked sharply.

"We're talking about winning!" Abby shot back. "I want to win every game!"

"Well, the first step to winning is paying attention, so try that for starters," Coach said. She smiled to show Abby that she wasn't really angry. "The Wellington team will be here in a few minutes, so let's start talking strategy. Our first line will be Emiko, Sam, Sarah, Jessie, and Kim. I will move other players in and out as I see fit, and then at halftime, I'll set a solid second line."

Coach Marshall continued to talk, but Abby felt too numb to be able to hear her properly. Her stomach was in knots. Why hadn't Coach Marshall chosen her for the first line? Why had she picked Sarah?

I'm a way better player than Sarah is, Abby thought bitterly.

Coach began to talk about the strengths and weaknesses of last year's Wellington team, but Abby only half-heard her. She couldn't believe that she and Sarah were being treated differently. *I've been trying so hard,* she thought.

When the Wellington players entered the gym, Coach waved at them and then told the Hawks to start their warm-up. Abby did as she was told.

"Want to work on our passing drills?" Sarah asked.

"Nope. I'm doing free throws," Abby responded, stepping neatly around her sister.

"Fine then," Sarah said.

I don't care if I've hurt her feelings, Abby thought, but it wasn't really true. *It's not Sarah's fault Coach picked her and not me*, she realized. *I'm being mean to her for no reason.*

Abby stepped up to the line and focused on the net. Bounce, bounce, bounce. Bounce, bounce, bounce. She crouched, and then straightened up as she pushed the ball up and away. It sailed through the air and fell neatly through the net. Smiling, she jogged over to retrieve her ball.

After a couple more great throws, she looked around for someone else to practice with. Sarah stood nearby, working on passing with Emiko and Sam. She was practicing with the team captains! Emiko and Sam had their backs to Abby, too, so she knew that neither of them had seen her terrific free throws.

"Don't waste practice time — ever," Coach Marshall warned Abby as she walked by. "The game's about to start and you're staring into space. I need you to be alert, even if you aren't one of the starting players."

Abby nodded miserably and headed for the home team's bench. She noticed her parents in the crowd on the bleachers and gave them a sunny wave so they wouldn't know how upset she was. As Sarah took her place out on the court, Abby slumped onto the bench.

"Hey, Abby," said Marta, the girl sitting next to her. "Isn't this exciting? Our first game is about to start!"

"Too bad we have to watch it from the bench," said Abby.

Marta laughed. "Don't worry. It's going to be a long game. We'll get played." She drank from her water bottle and wiped her mouth with the back of her hand.

Out on the court, the two team centres were getting prepared for the jump ball.

When the game started, Sam neatly won possession and passed the ball to Sarah. Abby watched as her sister moved around the court, jockeying for position and outsmarting her check. Sarah looked good — but Abby knew she could have played just as well, if not better. She slid to the very edge of the bench, jiggling one leg impatiently.

As the minutes ticked by and the players switched off, Abby realized that Coach had no intention of playing her. Her mood darkened as Sarah flopped down on the bench next to her and gulped down most of the water from her bottle.

"Wow, am I tired!" Sarah said. "It's hard to keep up." She took another long drink and then shook out her sweaty ponytail and redid it.

"You're doing great," Abby told her miserably. "I want to get out there too."

"I'm sure it won't be long," Sarah said. Just then Coach signaled Sarah back onto the court as Jessie headed for the sidelines.

"Seriously? Again?" Sarah muttered. She took a final swig of water and jogged back onto the court. Abby scowled.

Abby's turn to play finally came in the last two minutes of the game — she almost couldn't believe it when Coach waved her onto the court. Wellington had possession, so Abby worked hard to block her check.

"You're not getting past me," she told the girl firmly.

"Oh, I will," Abby's check replied, and tried to step past Abby. When that didn't work, she tried to pass to a teammate, but Abby jumped up high and plucked the ball away, passing to Emiko as the clock ran down. Abby's check darted away and Abby charged after her.

It wasn't the game of Abby's dreams, in which she scored basket after basket while her family cheered — but she stayed close to her check until the buzzer sounded and didn't give her any openings. The Hawks won!

"All right! We did it!" Marta shouted, clapping Abby on the shoulder. "It feels so great to win!"

"It would feel better if we'd been on the court a bit more," Abby replied, but she managed to smile at Marta.

"Hey, cheer up," Marta said. "A win's a win, right?" She headed over to the centre of the gym where all of the Hawks were jumping around high-fiving each other. Abby followed her, joining in on the tail end of the celebration. Eventually both teams lined up for the post-game handshakes, reciting the standard, "Good game, good game." Abby looked over at her parents in the bleachers and waved at them before she jogged back to the change room.

"Great job, Abby," said Sarah, flopping down next to her and kicking off her shoes. Sarah's hair was all messed up and sweat ran down her face in wide streaks starting above both temples. Abby glanced at her own reflection in the mirror and noticed that she looked as if she'd barely been exercising.

Abby smiled. "Thanks," she said, then grudgingly added, "You did great too."

Coach Marshall stepped into the centre of the change room. "Good work, girls! We're off to a winning start. We have an away game against Central on Thursday, so I'll see you back here tomorrow afternoon for practice."

When Coach turned to leave the change room, Abby jumped up to follow her. "Wait for me, okay?" she asked Sarah. "I just want to ask Coach something."

"Okay, but hurry up. Mom and Dad are waiting to drive us home."

"I won't be long." Abby pushed the change-room door open and jogged after her coach.

"Can I ask you something, Coach Marshall?" she called.

"Sure, Abby. What is it?"

"Well . . ." Abby hesitated, and then blurted out her question. "Why did you play Sarah so much during the game, and me barely at all?" she asked. "I thought I was as least as good as my sister is. What am I doing wrong?"

Coach Marshall smiled. "You aren't doing anything wrong, Abby," she said. "As far as I can tell, you're doing everything right. You're actually a stronger player than your sister is and that's why you sat on the bench today while she played."

"I don't understand. You didn't let me play much because you think I'm a *good* player?"

"Exactly. We need to come out strong and stay strong throughout the season. So my job as your coach is to make sure everyone's ready for that. Sarah, Jessie, and Kim have all of the skills to make them excellent players, but they don't have the confidence on the court that you have. I need them to get some practice as quickly as possible so they can get up to speed."

All Abby could manage to say was "Oh." A smile spread across her face and Coach Marshall smiled back.

"You're talented, Abby," she said. "Don't worry about today's game. Just keep showing up to practices and games, and you'll get your time on the court. See you tomorrow." She waved and headed down the hall toward her office.

Abby leaned against the wall, beaming happily. *I wish I could tell Mom and Dad what Coach said,* she thought. *It would hurt Sarah's feelings, though — and Mom and Dad wouldn't understand anyway. They'd probably just say I shouldn't be so worried about being the best.*

She decided to keep the good news all to herself.

6 PRACTICE MAKES PERFECT

The next afternoon most of the girls were sore and slow after the game, but Coach Marshall had no interest in hearing them complain. "Let's get started," she said briskly. "Break into groups of three, one ball per group. Today's all about shooting." Sarah ran up to Abby and Sam came over to join them. Each time Coach Marshall blew her whistle, three girls started across the gym, passing back and forth until the centre took a shot on net. "When you finish, switch your centre and start again," Coach Marshall reminded them.

"I can barely move after yesterday," Sarah muttered.

"What, you can't handle a bit of exercise?" Abby teased.

Sarah shot the ball at her sister's midsection. "I guess you wouldn't know what I'm talking about, Abby. You didn't play much yesterday, did you?"

"Easy, you two," Sam warned. "We're here to be a team, remember?" She was half-joking, but Sarah and Abby clammed up immediately. They didn't want to get on the team captain's bad side.

Abby moved to the starting point, flanked by Sam and Sarah. The whistle blew and she dribbled toward the basket, pivoted, and made a chest pass to Sam. Sam passed quickly to Sarah and Sarah dribbled a few times before bounce-passing back to Abby. As soon as Abby made the jump shot, she knew it was going in. It just felt right. She sunk the basket and beamed as everyone cheered for her.

"Nice work!" Sarah shouted. The three of them took their place at the back of the line, switching off so Sam could play centre.

"Sorry I teased you — you're doing great," Sarah told Abby. "That shot was amazing."

"Thanks."

They set out again, flanking Sam as she dribbled, pivoted, and passed. Her shot was completely different from Abby's — more of a hook — but it went through the hoop cleanly. Abby clapped Sam on the shoulder and exclaimed, "Nice one!"

They worked their way through the line again and then Sarah took her turn as centre. Her style was looser than Abby's or Sam's, and she almost seemed to hurl the ball at the basket, but it went in.

Next, Coach had them work on endurance, running laps around the gym. When the girls were all good and tired, she allowed a two-minute break, and then set everyone up to play keep-away, using the same groupings as the earlier drill.

Abby stood between Sarah and Sam and tried to intercept as they moved the ball back and forth. After a few exchanges, Sarah fumbled a pass. Abby lunged for the ball and neatly dribbled it away from Sarah.

"Nice, Abby and Sarah," Coach Marshall said. "You two can really anticipate each other on the court. I can see you've spent a lot of time playing together."

Abby grinned. "You should play us on a line together!" she said excitedly.

Coach Marshall nodded thoughtfully and walked away.

"That'd be great if she did that, wouldn't it?" asked Sarah eagerly.

"It would," Abby agreed. If she could get on a line with Sarah, they could show the coach how well they played together — and maybe Abby could manage to outshine Sarah a little. Once Coach Marshall saw how important Abby's skills were to winning the season, she'd be sure to give her the chance to play. After all, Coach had promised it wouldn't be long until Abby got out on the court.

7 BETTER THAN YOU?

Sure enough, Coach Marshall put Sarah and Abby on the starting line for the Thursday afternoon away game against Central. "I've decided not to hold you back," she told Abby. "I want to see how you do on a line with your sister. You know each other's strengths and weaknesses so well that you really complement each other's play. I'm looking forward to seeing what you can bring to the game together."

"Thanks, Coach!" said Abby, bouncing up and down ever so slightly in her court shoes. "We're going to *destroy* Central!"

"Good stuff, Abby . . . just remember to focus! First comes the hard work, then comes winning," Coach Marshall warned with a smile.

As they took their positions on either side of Emiko, Abby caught a glimpse of their parents and Lisa sitting on the bleachers just behind the home team's bench. She felt a burst of pride as she imagined how impressed they'd all be when they saw her play.

Emiko poised to spring up for the ball. She lost the tipoff, but the opposing centre fumbled her first pass and Sarah ended up getting possession. Sarah dribbled to the net and then passed to Emiko, whose check boxed her in just outside the key.

"Over here!" Abby shouted at Emiko. Abby's check from the Central team was right up in her face, but Abby still reached her arms high as she tried to maneuver into a better scoring position. Emiko glanced over at Abby, but passed the ball back to Sarah instead. When Sarah sunk a long shot to open the scoring, the crowd cheered and whistled in appreciation. Abby noticed her parents and Lisa on their feet, clapping wildly. "Good one, Sarah!" their mother shouted.

Abby clapped and gave Sarah a thumbs-up, but as she ran down the court, she was determined to get the ball and show everyone what *she* could do. She got the ball from Emiko and sped down the court.

"I'm open! Abby, I'm open!" Sarah shouted.

"Over here, Abby!" Emiko called.

Abby ignored them both. She powered her way around the court, made a perfect layup, and scored two more points for the Hawks. Applause filled her ears. A few minutes later, Sarah passed to Abby and then moved into a good shooting position.

"Pass it back, Abby!" Sarah called. Instead, Abby headed toward the basket for a second time.

"Abby, throw it to Sarah!" Emiko called. Abby

pretended not to hear. She could see Sarah waving at her but all she could think about was the basket, which she could barely see through the waving arms of her very tall opponent.

"PASS THE BALL, ABBY!" Coach Marshall shouted, but it was too late. Abby lost the ball to her check and, after some fast teamwork, the Central girls had their first basket of the game.

"Nice work, superstar," Abby's check said mockingly.

"Whatever," Abby shot back. "Two points is nothing. We're going to win this game."

The other girl made a face. "Not the way you're playing."

The ball came their way and both girls leapt for it, but Abby was quicker. She wanted to shoot, but she knew she was unlikely to score from halfway down the court. Dribbling and pivoting away from the other girl, she studied her options.

Sarah looked as though she had the best chance of getting a basket, but Kim was closest to Abby and she had a fairly weak check. At the same time, Sam had just come on, so she wasn't as tired as the rest of the girls. Sarah was definitely the best choice — but Abby chose Sam. Sam passed to Kim, and Kim bounced the ball off the rim while trying for a three-pointer.

"Abby, what are you doing?" hissed Sarah as she ran past.

"Trying to score," Abby muttered.

She heard someone shout her name and glanced toward the bench to see Coach Marshall waving her off the court. Marta stood on the sidelines, ready to replace her. Abby charged into the centre of play instead, calling out for the ball. *I messed up that play . . . now I need to get us some points*, she thought. Jessie passed it to her and Abby hurled the ball toward the basket. It hit the backboard hard and the sound echoed in the gym. The Hawks all looked shocked.

"Coach wants you off, Abby," Marta called.

"Yeah, go and study up on how to play the game," said Abby's new check, a shortish blond girl. "You're *terrible*! You're such a bad player that you're helping *our* team win!"

Abby stomped off the court, horrified that she'd been tossed from the game in front of her parents and Lisa. *I'm completely humiliated*, she thought. She plunked down onto the bench and grabbed her water bottle.

"You can put your warm-ups on, Abby," Coach Marshall said. "I won't be sending you back out. You need to think about what it means to be a team player."

"I thought you wanted players who care about winning!"

Coach Marshall sat down next to Abby. She met her gaze for a long time before she spoke.

"I'm not sure where you got that idea from, Abby," she said gently. "I am looking for players who can work toward a goal — as a *team*. Anyone can hog the ball and run around on the court with it. It takes teamwork to succeed. All you did out there today was mess up your teammates and show Central our weaknesses as a squad. We should be ahead in this game, but now we're struggling to catch up."

She tapped Abby on the shoulder. "Don't be angry, Abby, be realistic. Think about what I've told you, and use our next practice to show me that you know what I'm talking about."

8 WHAT WERE YOU THINKING?

"Abby, are you crazy? What were you doing out there?" Sarah grabbed Abby's arm as they headed into the change room. "I thought we were going to have this fun game together, and then you totally —"

"I totally screwed things up. Yeah, I *know*, Sarah. I know you think I'm an idiot. Just leave me alone."

Abby stormed over to her locker and quickly undressed, pulling her towel around her. Sarah followed as Abby darted over to a shower stall.

"I just don't understand why you didn't pass to me."

"I wanted to shoot," Abby said miserably. "I thought I had a clear shot, okay? I just wanted to win."

"Well I felt like you just didn't want me to have the ball. I was standing there wide open, *yelling* for you to pass, and you ignored me."

"You're not the only one," Emiko said as she walked past. "Abby ignored me too."

"I'm sorry," Abby muttered. "I don't know what I was thinking." *This is so different from what I imagined,* she thought. *Everyone is paying attention to me, but it's not because I did well. It's because I played so badly.*

"Hey, Abby? We lost by sixteen points. Here's an idea for you — maybe the next time the *co-captain of the team* shouts for you to pass the ball, you could do me a favour and *listen*," Emiko called from the next stall.

Abby looked over at Sarah wearily.

"She won't stay mad," Sarah reassured her.

"Was I really that terrible?"

Sarah shrugged and said quietly, "I was super excited that we got to play together, but you didn't even look at me on the court. Then you got yourself kicked out of the game. Being on a team with you isn't so great after all."

"What did you expect? I told you from the start, this whole *team* thing isn't what I'm good at."

"I thought we'd have fun. I thought it would be more like when we play at home on the driveway, except even more fun because the games would be *real*."

"Sorry I disappointed you," Abby said. She turned on the water with a quick, jerky motion. As Sarah closed the curtain and walked away, Abby shut her eyes and wished she was somewhere else.

★★★

"Do you actually enjoy basketball, Abby?" her dad asked her the next morning at breakfast.

Abby squirmed uncomfortably. She'd ignored several texts from Lisa the night before, asking her if everything was okay.

"Of course I do, Dad," she replied.

"Hmm."

"What do you mean, *hmm*?"

"Well, when the game started, I noticed that all of the other kids seemed to be enjoying themselves, but you looked different. You almost looked angry."

"I was probably just focused on the game. You know, working super hard, trying to find some openings to score," Abby said cautiously. "At our first practice, Coach Marshall said the number-one goal for this team is winning."

"I don't remember that at all!" Sarah said. Her eyebrows were raised in surprise as she looked at Abby. "She said —"

"She said we *need* to win back the championship," Abby interrupted.

Sarah crossed her arms in front of her. "All I know is that you don't win by doing your own thing," she said. "The team still gets the points if you let someone else sink the basket, you know."

"Back up a bit," their dad said, his face concerned. "Abby, why do you think your coach's number-one goal is winning?"

"It's not just Coach Marshall's goal, it's the goal of the *school*," Abby said importantly. "Harewood needs to win back the district championship at all costs."

Sarah shook her head as she buttered herself another slice of toast. "I don't think that's what she said at all. I wouldn't even want to be on a team like that. We're supposed to be having fun."

"I agree with Sarah," their mom said. "School teams should be more about the teamwork than the end result." She leaned forward and smiled at Abby. "When I watched your game, I wasn't all that interested in the score. I came to see you play. You didn't seem to be enjoying yourself much, Abby. It bothered me that you didn't look happy."

Their dad nodded. "Don't worry so much about winning, Abby," he said gently. "Basketball is supposed to be fun — that's what I remember about playing on my high school team. Think about how much you and Sarah enjoy yourselves when you play out in the yard."

"Yeah, but . . ." Abby trailed off.

"I'm not trying to pick on you," her father said gently. "I just want to see the same happy look on your face when you play with the team as you do when you and Sarah play at home. If your coach has a problem with that, maybe Mom or I should have a talk with her."

"I think Coach Marshall wants us to be happy too, Dad." Sarah said. "When we tried out for the team, she talked about how much fun being on the Hawks was going to be."

Abby shot her sister a look. "Sure, gang up on me. Why do you have to criticize the way I play basketball?" She turned to her parents. "If you guys don't support the team, don't come to the games." Abby stood up abruptly and pushed herself from the table, scraping her chair on the floor.

Abby stalked up the stairs to her room. She couldn't believe how badly her plan had backfired. Secretly, she hoped her parents would follow her, but neither one of them did.

★★★

Abby waited until Sarah had left before sneaking back downstairs and out the door.

Lisa was already at their usual meeting place, sitting on her backpack and eating an apple while listening to her mp3 player. Abby grinned as she noticed her friend's artsy outfit — striped sleeves sticking out from under a plain black T-shirt, black-and-white-checked socks, silver sneakers, and a denim skirt. You couldn't help but notice Lisa in a crowd.

"Hey," said Lisa, sticking her mp3 player and ear buds into a side pocket on her pack.

"Hi," Abby said back. They started toward school in comfortable silence, Lisa's sparkly sneakers and Abby's more practical blue-and-white runners crunching through the autumn leaves.

"So, what was that all about yesterday?" asked Lisa after they'd walked for a while. "It was a bit shocking to watch you play."

Abby groaned. "Did I really look *that* bad?"

"You looked like you had no idea there were other players on your team," Lisa said bluntly.

"Great."

"Don't worry," Lisa reassured her. "It's early in the year, and it was only one game. There's lots of time to work at it."

Abby felt her temper flare. "I don't feel like I should have to work at it. I was only trying to play my best game and beat Central. I just got too focused on myself. I wanted to be the best one out there."

"Did you want to be the best one out there, or did you just want to be better than Sarah?"

Abby glared at her.

"Don't get mad at me for asking," Lisa said hurriedly. "Just listen for a minute. I watched the whole game and a lot of the time, it looked as if you were purposely keeping the ball away from Sarah."

Abby sighed. "Sarah is super good at everything. I'm good at basketball — or at least I thought I was. I know she doesn't do it on purpose, but I feel like she's always in the spotlight. She's prettier, more outgoing, funnier, builds cool props with Dad, has a million new friends . . ." Abby trailed off. As they passed the coffee shop, Fresh Ground, Abby glanced in the window.

There was Sarah, surrounded by friends and spooning whipped cream out of a large steaming mug.

"I feel like basketball is my one chance at being better than she is at something, so I care about it more than she does," Abby admitted. "She's the one who suggested joining the team, but for her, it's just one more thing to do. For me, it's *the* thing."

"You're better at lots of things than Sarah is, though," Lisa reasoned. "I don't think she's ever made the honour roll in her life. Am I right?"

"Yeah . . . but that's different. School's such a small part of things."

"That's what you think. School is super important, and Sarah would love to be able to get the grades you do. She's told me that plenty of times."

"I know," Abby said.

"You're better at swimming than she is too."

"That's because she gave up on lessons. She's happy to dog paddle around."

"Face it — you're better at it. You're better at cooking too . . . and you're a way faster reader than Sarah is, and —"

Abby smiled. "Thanks for trying to make me feel better, Lees."

"Is it working?"

"Not really. All those things are true, but basketball is just different. I never thought of myself as the kind of person who could play on a team, but now I really want to be that person." Abby groaned in frustration. "I thought it would be a lot easier to figure out how to be good at it. When I play one-on-one, I know all the right moves, but I need to figure out how to put it together and play well on a team."

As they headed across the school lawn, Lisa put her arm around Abby. "Oh, Abby . . . Wait. I've got just the thing to make you feel better." Lisa pulled out her mp3 player and guided Abby onto a bench. "Listen to this new song with me before the bell rings?"

Abby laughed. "Is that your answer for everything?"

9 ABBY TAKES CHARGE

Not many girls said hello to Abby at practice that afternoon. She knew they were still upset about losing the game, but their unfriendliness made her feel like an outsider. To make matters worse, Sarah hadn't even shown up for practice — and hadn't bothered to warn Abby that she wouldn't be there.

"Where's your sister?" Coach Marshall asked as the warm-up was about to start.

Abby shrugged.

Coach frowned as she marked Sarah absent. "Well, when you see her, let her know that I expect players to have extremely good reasons for missing practices," she said. "This isn't some rec league."

"I know," said Abby. She felt some of the other girls looking at her and she forced herself to meet their eyes. Emiko glared at Abby and Abby glared back.

"Since we have some players who seemed a bit confused about passing in our last game, we'll start to-day's practice with a little review," Coach said. Groans echoed through the gym, but she waved off the girls' protests.

"Thanks a lot, Abby!" Emiko hissed.

Abby gave her a curt nod and turned back to the coach, who was explaining the first drill.

"We're going to play chase," Coach began. "You will go two by two down the court. One player will throw the ball down the court in front of the other player. That player will gain control of the ball and complete a layup. If player two does not catch the ball or it goes too far in front of her, then she passes back to player one so that she can take a shot. Line up in twos and we'll begin. Abby, Emiko, I'd like you two to go first." She tossed a basketball in Abby's direction.

As Abby ran to catch up to the bouncing ball, she heard Emiko call out, "Can I start with the ball, Coach? I might never see it again otherwise."

Abby winced. "Very funny," she said as she tossed the ball to Emiko.

"Emiko, I'd like that to be the last sarcastic remark you make at this practice," Coach Marshall said sternly. "Abby knows she has some work to do today. Am I correct?" She glanced at Abby and Abby nodded obediently. "Yes, Coach."

"Okay. Start when you hear my whistle. Three, two, one . . ."

At the whistle blast, Emiko pounded across the gym floor and hurled the ball in front of Abby — *way* in front of Abby. It was pretty clear that Emiko wanted her to miss the pass. Abby gave it a try anyway, thundering across the gym and catching up to the ball almost directly under the net. Her timing was off and the shot she made went wide. She retrieved the ball as Emiko jogged up.

"Nice try," Emiko said sweetly.

"Thanks," Abby said calmly. "Are you ready for your turn?"

She bolted across the court and Emiko chased her. Abby didn't try to mess up Emiko's turn; she just moved the ball up the court and shot it in front of Emiko as she'd been told to do. Emiko completed a great layup.

"Excellent!" Coach Marshall called. "Okay, next pair, ready and GO!" As Jessie and Marta took off down the court, Abby and Emiko took their place at the back of the line.

"I don't understand why you didn't do that during the game yesterday," Emiko said, running an orange-polished fingernail through her short hair.

Abby shrugged. "I wasn't trying to screw up," she told Emiko. "I was trying to get points and I guess I was just thinking about my own strategy and stuff," she said, staring at the floor. "I feel bad. Sorry."

"Thanks for apologizing," Emiko said. "I'm sorry I have such a bad temper. After the game Sam told me I should cool down a bit and then we should both talk with you, but I didn't listen to her. I'm still so mad at you, Abby. We could have won that game!"

"I know," Abby said quietly.

The drill was almost finished and several of the girls started to clap as the final two players finished up.

"Okay," said Coach, glancing over at Emiko and Abby. "Lesson learned? Or do we need another passing drill?"

"Lesson learned," Abby piped up. Some of her teammates gave her skeptical looks, but Emiko stuck up for her. "We can move on, Coach," she said.

"Okay then, time to scrimmage. Emiko, why don't you and Sam figure out the lineups."

Sam and Emiko moved off to the side of the group. "I get Abby," Abby heard Emiko say. She knew that Emiko would want her to keep passing the ball no matter what, so when the scrimmage started, that's exactly what she did. Except for one basket, Abby kept giving up the ball to other players so they could shoot. When Coach Marshall blew the whistle to end the match, Abby's team had won — only by two baskets, but it was still a win.

"Thanks for working hard today," Coach said to the group with a smile. "I have a lot more confidence in you girls than I did yesterday." She checked her watch and then kept talking.

"Before you leave, we need to talk about fundraising to pay for your uniforms," she said. "We have to make about a thousand dollars to pay back the school. Principal Baxter and I want the team to take charge of this, so what I'm looking for today is a player or players who can plan out the fundraising campaign."

"What do we need to do?" Marta asked.

"The person or people who volunteer will need to set up two or three fundraisers and make sure there are enough players to run them," Coach explained. "I'm willing to help you out, and to take the money you earn to the bank for you, but I don't want to get too involved with the planning."

"I'll do it!" Abby blurted out.

Everyone turned to look at her.

"Are you sure, Abby?" Sam asked. "It sounds like a lot of work for one person."

"I think it sounds like fun," Abby answered. It sounded scary, too, but it seemed like a good way to socialize more — and a good way to show Coach Marshall and her teammates that she was committed to the Hawks.

"Does anyone have any problem with Abby taking this job?" Coach Marshall asked. No one said anything, so she nodded at Abby. "All right, it's yours," she said. "You'll probably need to have your first fundraiser in the next couple of weeks. The sooner we can pay for the uniforms, the happier the principal will be."

"I already have an idea," said Abby. "I want to have a car wash here at school, before the weather gets too cold. We should do it on a Saturday." A couple of the girls groaned.

"Why Saturday? Why not choose a school night?" Jessie asked.

"We'll get more cars on a Saturday, and we can start early," Abby said.

Coach nodded. "That sounds like a great way to start," she said. "Abby, how about if you and I check with Principal Baxter right after practice. We can probably set things up for a week from this Saturday."

"Okay," said Abby, resisting the impulse to do a little dance. Coach liked her idea! This new job was going to put Abby right back in the centre of things. The day hadn't started out too well, but now things were looking better.

★★★

Forty minutes later, Abby zipped her coat, shouldered her pack, and set out for home with an ear-to-ear grin. Principal Baxter had loved her idea, and had given her permission to organize a car wash for a week from Saturday. She couldn't wait to tell her parents about her new responsibility.

"Hi, Abby."

She turned to see Sarah walking up beside her. With surprise, Abby noticed that Sarah was quite dressed up in a navy dress and tights, with her hair pulled back in a twist. She had her backpack on too, and she was carrying a purple folder thick with papers.

"How come you skipped practice?" asked Abby. "What's with the dress?"

"I just felt like dressing up today," Sarah said vaguely.

"Well, you do look nice, but you would have looked a lot nicer in shorts and court shoes," Abby said. "Coach was wondering where you were."

"I'll talk to her tomorrow . . . I just had a meeting for a class project. I couldn't miss it."

"You should have let Coach know ahead of time."

Sarah sighed. "Abby, I would have let her know if I'd realized the meeting would take this long! I'm sorry."

"Whatever you say." Abby paused, and then asked, "Do you want to know about the first fundraiser for our uniforms?"

"When is it?"

"It's a week from Saturday in the parking lot by the gym. It's a car wash. Can you come?"

"Of course. I'll let Coach know when I talk to her tomorrow."

"Oh, you can just let me know," said Abby, tossing her hair importantly. "I'm the fundraising coordinator."

"*You* are?" Sarah couldn't hide her surprise.

"Is there something wrong with that?"

"Well, it's just . . . I thought everyone was kind of mad at you, that's all."

"Well, if you'd bothered to show up to practice, you would've seen me do an awesome drill with *Emiko* and a great scrimmage too. No one was mad at me by the end of practice, and when I volunteered to handle all of our fundraisers, everyone agreed that I could do it."

Sarah looked startled. "You're planning all the fundraisers? Not just this one?"

"All of them. I get to come up with all of the ideas and organize the volunteers. It's all up to me," Abby beamed. "I'm super excited."

"Well, umm, that's great," Sarah said. "It sounds like tons of work though. Can I help? It would be so easy for us to work on this together. I totally would have volunteered to help you if I'd been at practice."

Abby could tell that her sister really meant it. She considered saying yes, but decided against it. *She'll just overshadow me, the way she always does*, Abby thought. *Before long she'll be at the centre of things getting all of the praise while I get pushed aside.*

"Thanks, but this is my job," Abby told her. "I volunteered to do it and I really want to do it by myself."

Sarah looked disappointed. "Okay, fine," she replied.

Abby felt bad — but not bad enough to change her mind. She and Sarah walked the rest of the way home in silence.

10 CAR WASH!

"Sarah, could you move it? We're going to be late." Exasperated, Abby turned to wait for her sister.

"Sure, sorry. I guess I grabbed too much stuff and didn't organize it very well." Sarah dropped the two buckets, squeegee, rubber gloves, oversized sponges, and sprayer she was carrying and bent down to tie her shoe. Abby thought that Sarah looked really cute in her new jeans, T-shirt, and hoodie. You'd never know that she'd only woken up fifteen minutes earlier. *I wish I could look that good without trying*, she thought.

With a sigh of frustration, Abby set down the several homemade posters and car-washing gear that she was carrying and walked back half a block to where her sister was crouched on the sidewalk. She stacked up Sarah's buckets and organized the rest of the equipment inside the top one.

"Sorry, Abby, I can do that," said Sarah. She straightened up and took the buckets from her. "Can I carry some posters for you too?"

"I've got them."

They walked for a block or so and then Abby asked, "Do you want to wash cars first this morning, or carry the advertising signs, or scrimmage? I thought it would be fun to have some girls playing basketball throughout the day, so people can see the team in action. It might make them want to donate more money."

"That makes sense," Sarah said. "I could scrimmage . . . or actually, it might be fun to do the advertising. I like the idea of waving at cars and holding up a sign."

As they rounded the corner, they saw that most of the team was already gathered in the parking lot, putting up brightly coloured signs and setting up orange road cones to designate car-wash spaces.

Abby ran over to the telephone pole by the parking lot entrance, where Emiko and Jessie were duct-taping a huge orange sign. "Car Wash by Donation," it read. "Support the Harewood Junior Hawks."

"That looks terrific," Abby said approvingly. She pulled a poster out of one of her buckets. "Mine just say Car Wash."

"Works for me," Emiko said. "I like the block lettering. It shows up really well."

Abby grinned. "Thanks. I thought we could take turns holding these ones and waving the cars in. We could stand up the street a ways so they have time to slow down and turn into the parking lot. Sarah already volunteered to take the first shift."

"Looks like she's already in position," Emiko said. Abby looked up to see her sister standing half a block away from the school, happily waving at passing cars.

"Car wash today!" Sarah shouted.

Abby walked over to her with one of the signs.

"Here," she said, handing the sign to Sarah. "This will make it easier." Sarah nodded her thanks and Abby walked back down to the parking lot and checked her watch — two minutes to nine.

"Thanks for coming, everyone," Abby said, after gathering the team around her. "Sarah's up on the sidewalk getting people's attention — I have a couple more signs if anyone wants to join her. We'll need two or three people up on the road at all times, and I thought the rest of us could split into two groups. Half of us can play basketball on the outdoor court over there, half of us can wash cars, and we can trade a couple of times an hour. If it gets really busy, we can all pitch in and wash cars. I can hang onto the money — it will be my responsibility if anything happens to it."

Emiko smiled. "Thanks for planning this out, Abby," she said. "I'll take one of your signs and help Sarah for the first little while." Abby handed her one of the large cardboard squares and Emiko strode toward Sarah.

"I'll take one too," said Sam. She took Abby's last handmade sign and followed Emiko. *Oh great*, Abby thought. *Sarah's going to spend the next few hours hanging out with the team captains! I thought this fundraising job would help me socialize more, but I just don't have the natural charm that Sarah does.*

Abby couldn't believe how easily her sister got things to go her way. She hadn't even gotten in trouble for the practice she'd missed. Coach Marshall had just asked her to let her know about any other meetings she had, *in case they ran late.* Abby was sure she would never have received such special treatment.

Abby took a deep breath and turned her focus back to the car wash, "Okay, I'll set up the hose," she told the group of girls gathered around her. "You guys can decide who wants to play basketball and who wants to help me wash cars."

As she jogged over to the side of the school to connect the hose, Abby snuck a glance at Sarah, Emiko, and Sam. The three of them stood laughing and talking as they waved at passing vehicles. *By the end of the day, they'll all be best friends,* Abby thought miserably.

Just then, Abby's parents' car turned into the parking lot with a friendly double-honk at Sarah, Sam, and Emiko. Abby knew her parents were on their way downtown to drop off some props for a play set in ancient Greece — dismantled, weathered-looking columns and arches were piled high in the back of the station wagon.

"Yay!" Sam shouted. "We have our first customers!"

Abby waved at her parents and guided the family car into a marked parking space. She shook some soap into one of her buckets and turned the hose on.

Abby's mom leaned out the driver's side window to hand her a twenty. "What, no lineup yet?" she teased.

"Sarah's working on it. Hop out and we'll get started." Abby pulled the hose out of the full bucket and handed the end to Jessie, who began soaking down the car as soon as Abby's parents were out of the way. Abby soaked a sponge in the soapy water as more girls came over to join in.

"Look who's here!" Abby's dad said, pointing. Abby looked up to see Lisa and her family turning in to the parking lot too. Coach Marshall's truck was right behind them, waiting to turn in.

"It pays to have supportive friends and family," Abby replied, smiling at her parents. She guided Lisa's father into the next parking spot.

★★★

By eleven, things were going full swing. Business had been steady all morning — Lisa had even stayed to help after a rush of vehicles arrived in the first few minutes. Even Coach helped out washing cars for a while, before heading into the school to catch up on some work.

"I think we've raised about five hundred dollars so far," Abby told Lisa. The two of them had taken over the signs and Sarah and Sam had taken a shift playing basketball. Both girls were in uniform and the shiny fabric looked terrific as they passed the ball back and forth in the late-morning sunlight.

"That's great," Lisa said. "I think it really helps that people can see the uniforms."

The sound of a baby crying pierced the air as a car pulled up alongside Lisa and Abby. Two women sat in front, and Abby could see an infant in the back, wriggling around in a rear-facing car seat positioned between two older kids. The tired-looking woman sitting on the passenger side reached out the window and handed Abby ten dollars.

"We don't have time to stop, but we want to support you," she said. "Good luck." The car rolled away.

"Wow," Lisa said as she waved at the vehicle. "That sure was nice."

"Totally. It would have been easy to just drive by. I'm going to run down quickly and tell everyone about this. It will make them feel good."

"Okay, Abby, I have to take off. Will you guys be okay?"

"Sure. Thanks for helping, Lees."

Abby waved goodbye to Lisa and headed down the driveway, but the smile on her face faded as she noticed Sam and Sarah standing together and gossiping instead of playing basketball. Frustrated, she jogged over to them.

"What are you doing?" she asked. "You're supposed to be shooting baskets right now."

"We're just taking a break," replied Sarah.

"Taking breaks isn't helpful!"

"Abby, come on, this is going to be a long day," Sarah said. "You've done a great job of organizing things, but it's crazy to expect us to work all day long with no breaks. Relax! Come and hang out with us for a while."

"Relax? This is really important, Sarah! The school is counting on us to raise the money for our uniforms!"

Sarah shrugged and gave Abby a tight smile. "There's not much to do right now. We only have two cars and the other girls are handling it." She gave Abby a penetrating look. "Everything's fine."

Abby stormed over to the car-wash zone and picked up a sponge to help Emiko. A minute or two later, Sarah walked over to join her.

"Look, Abby," she said, picking up an oversized green sponge. "If it's really important to you for me to be busy, I can be busy."

"Oh *no*," Abby answered sarcastically. "We don't need any help around here, Sarah. *Relax!* Go back and enjoy your break!"

Sarah looked stunned. "Why are you being such a jerk?"

"Me? You're the one who isn't taking this fundraiser seriously!" Abby let all of her frustration with Sarah come out. She felt guilty about yelling at Sarah in front of the team, but she just couldn't stop herself. She was tired of Sarah getting special treatment.

"You aren't even taking the team seriously. You skipped practice and didn't even tell the coach where you were. You didn't even tell your own sister! We're all in this to win, but it seems like you're just along for the ride."

"I am totally taking this car-wash thing seriously . . . and I explained about the practice to you *and* Coach Marshall. What's your problem?" Sarah said, her voice shaking. Abby could tell that her sister was trying hard not to cry. Sarah threw the sponge into the nearest bucket and looked around at the girls watching them. "Thanks, Abby. Thanks a lot." She turned and walked away quickly.

Abby felt everyone's eyes on her, but even though she knew she'd hurt Sarah's feelings, she didn't run after her sister.

The twenty-something driver of the car Abby and Emiko were washing gave Abby a sympathetic look.

"That's too bad you lost a helper," she told them kindly, and wandered off to watch Sam and Kim play basketball.

"Wow," said Emiko. "That was harsh."

Abby shrugged. "She had it coming."

Emiko didn't answer. The two girls finished washing the car in silence. As another car pulled into its place, Emiko wandered over to the basketball hoop. "Can I trade off with one of you?" she asked Kim and Sam.

"No, I don't want to work with Abby," Abby heard

Kim say. "Can you believe she did that to her own *sister*? Sarah's the nicest girl on the team."

"I'm fine by myself, Emiko," Abby called. Emiko waved and threw her basketball jersey on over top of her shirt. Sam passed the ball and Emiko bounded up for a quick jump shot.

"It's nothing but net!" Sam yelled as the ball sailed through the hoop. "Good for you!" She scooped up the ball, began to dribble, and gestured for Kim and Emiko to join her. "Let's play some two-on-one."

The three girls sparred back and forth, fighting for the ball, practicing shots and rebounds. Abby kept to herself, washing cars in silence. Her enthusiasm for the fundraiser was totally gone.

"Abby, can we talk for a second?" Coach Marshall's voice startled Abby; she hadn't noticed the coach sitting on the concrete with her back against the outer gym wall. Abby nodded and the two of them walked toward the far end of the parking lot.

"I wanted to tell you that I watched you and Sarah having your spat earlier," Coach Marshall said. "Do you really think the five-minute break she took was unreasonable?"

Abby gazed down at her feet. "Probably not," she admitted. "It just made me so mad to turn around and see her fooling around. I took this day so seriously."

"Well, you've done a great job, but it's too bad you had to alienate your sister. Sarah put in a lot of hard work. She did a great job encouraging people to come to the car wash, and she washed several cars before she started playing basketball. She may be your sister, but she's your teammate too. I didn't like seeing you blow up at Sarah for something so small."

"I'm sorry," Abby said.

"Thank you, Abby. It would be nice if you said that to Sarah later as well." She smiled and placed her hand on Abby's right shoulder. "You're a terrific player with a lot of drive and skill, and I know you worked hard today. I suppose I could have praised you for that before criticizing the way you treated Sarah. Just remember, everyone deserves to be treated with respect."

"Thank you," Abby said. She felt like crying. The day had started out so well, but here she was again, apologizing for her behaviour when she'd only been trying to do a good job for the team. She was getting tired of messing things up, but she wasn't sure how to change things.

11 ABBY'S NEW GAME

Abby waited by Sarah's locker for a while before Monday's after-school home game. When her sister didn't show up, she made her way to the gym alone. *She probably left without me*, she thought sadly.

Sarah had barely spoken to her since the fundraiser. Abby had tried to take Coach Marshall's advice, but when she'd apologized to Sarah for losing her temper, Sarah had replied "Okay, whatever." Then she ended the conversation by turning on her mp3 player and pressing the ear buds firmly into her ears.

As Abby sat putting on her court shoes, she noticed Sarah wasn't in the change room. She kept her eye on the door, but at warm-up time, Sarah still hadn't appeared. Abby felt a bit worried, but she forced herself to act as though nothing was bothering her. *Sarah probably had another meeting she just didn't bother telling anybody about*, she told herself. A few minutes later she overheard Coach Marshall talking with Sam and Emiko.

"Sarah won't be here today. She had another

appointment," Coach Marshall told them. "I know you were counting on her to play on your first line."

"We can play Abby," Emiko said. "I think she'll do okay."

Okay? Abby couldn't believe what she'd just heard. Sarah had *permission* to miss the game? Abby was only going to play on the first line because Sarah wasn't around? Sarah didn't even show up, but for some reason, she was getting special treatment from the coach and team captains. What could Sarah be doing that was more important than the game?

"Hey, Abby," Emiko called. "Are you ready to start?"

Emiko, Sam, and Coach Marshall all looked at Abby expectantly. Abby nearly said something sarcastic in response, but she decided not to. "You bet!" she called agreeably.

After a quick team cheer, Abby got into position next to Sam and glanced out into the bleachers. She spotted her parents and Lisa. Abby felt great knowing they were there. *I wish Sarah was here too*, she thought. She shook her head angrily and pushed the thought from her mind. Sarah obviously wasn't interested enough to show up.

The Harbour View players took their places and the girl across from Abby smirked.

"Ready to get schooled?" she asked.

Abby kept her cool. Instead of freaking out, she calmly replied, "We'll see who gets schooled today."

The girl scoffed, but Abby just kept smiling, aware that her opponent was trying to get a rise out of her.

Sam lost the tipoff and Abby immediately found herself on the defensive. Her check was a good player but Abby kept up.

"You won't be scoring much tonight," she told her opponent.

"Whatever," the other girl replied, but every time she tried to fake Abby out, Abby stuck with her. The girl ended her shift with no scoring chances.

"Nice work, Abby," Coach Marshall called.

Abby got possession from her new check and passed to Jessie, who moved down the court and passed to Sam. Sam took a shot, and when it rebounded, Abby was there to put it in.

"Way to go, Abby!" she heard her father shout. Abby headed back up the court with her check, watching for openings and taking note of her teammates' positions. She played for a while longer, and then Coach Marshall called her off for a rest.

"Great work," Coach Marshall said as Abby mopped her forehead with a towel. She'd never had such a good game with the Hawks — and she realized that she was having fun too.

A few minutes later, Coach Marshall sent Abby back in and she quickly got the ball. She headed to the net and set up her shot, but her check fouled her mid-lay-up. Abby thought her shot might go in, but it bounced off the rim and she went to the free-throw line.

When she bounced the ball, it sounded like thunder in Abby's ears. She concentrated on the feel of the ball on her palms and the gym floor beneath her feet. Once she felt calm, she opened her eyes, crouched, and shot. It was good.

The fast pace continued, and the Junior Hawks hung onto their lead.

Abby worked hard against her check. She blocked several shots that she could tell the other girl thought were going in.

"You're like a mosquito — so annoying!" Abby's check complained. "Just go away!" Abby grinned. Moments later, she stole the ball and passed to Sam. Sam passed back to her, but Abby only touched the ball long enough to tip it to Emiko.

Emiko chanced a three-pointer — and sunk it!

"That was AWESOME!" Abby shouted. She caught a glimpse of her original check on the home-team bench. The girl's face was grim.

I guess we schooled you, Abby thought.

When the final buzzer sounded, the Hawks had won the game by eight points. Abby and her team-mates gathered near the bench to cheer and high-five each other.

"Excellent game, everyone," Coach Marshall said. "That was really great teamwork."

"You're a totally different player when your sister's

not on the court," Marta teased, elbowing Abby in the ribs.

"What do you mean?" asked Abby.

"Well, you don't like to pass the ball much when Sarah's around," Marta said knowingly. "I think you've got a bit of sibling rivalry going on there."

"Gee, do you think so?" Jessie snickered.

Abby felt unsure. She noticed that Coach Marshall had been listening, so she moved closer to her and asked, "Do Sarah and I play well together?"

"You do . . . when you pair off against each other in practice," Coach answered thoughtfully. "You do a great job one-on-one. When you're on a line together, though, you tend to forget how to pass."

"Do you mean both of us?"

Coach Marshall shook her head. "I only notice it in you. Sometimes it's like there are two different games happening on the court — the Hawks versus our opponent, and you versus your sister. You're extremely concerned about keeping up with Sarah. That can be a good thing — as long as you remember to be a team player too."

Sarah makes me push myself, Abby thought. *That's how I stay motivated — I need to play better than she does. It's just the way I feel.*

★★★

"Great game!" Abby's mom called as Abby walked out of the change room.

"You looked terrific," her dad chimed in. "Hey, Lisa had to leave, but she said to give you this." Her dad enveloped her in a huge bear hug.

"Thanks, you guys." Abby laughed. She beamed as she noticed how proud her parents were. "I had a great time today. I hope I get to play on the starting line more often."

"Oh, I'm sure you will," her mom said. Together they walked out into the school parking lot.

"Do you think Sarah's finished?" Abby's dad asked.

"Probably pretty soon," her mom replied. "She said she'd come out the theatre entrance, so we may as well drive over."

"Makes sense to me," said Abby's dad. They all climbed into the car and drove partway around the school. Abby's dad parked across from the theatre entrance.

"Um, will one of you tell me what's going on?" asked Abby. "Where's Sarah? Why did she skip our game?"

"Sarah is in a meeting with the theatre club," her dad said, surprised. "She didn't tell you about it? She's interested in making props for the winter play. It's a pirate theme."

"It will be so exciting if she's chosen," Abby's mom said happily. "Creating all of the pirate props will be such an experience."

"I can't believe she's interested in taking on a whole play herself," Abby's dad added. "It's so great to see her come into her own. She's tinkered around in the shop for years, helping me out, but this is different." He smiled. "Maybe she'll let *me* help *her*!"

"I had no idea," Abby said quietly.

"Really?" her dad looked at her closely. "This is her second meeting with the club."

"It's the first I've heard of it," said Abby. She thought back to the day Sarah missed basketball practice. She'd been quite dressed up when she and Abby met up afterward, and she'd been carrying a bundle of papers — probably a script. That must have been the day she'd had her interview with the club. Sarah had kept a secret from her — she'd even lied to keep Abby from knowing the truth.

"What about basketball?" Abby demanded. "Making props for a play is going to take up a ton of time. Sarah's a Junior Hawk! She needs to be focused!"

"I think Sarah is capable of making her own decisions about how she spends her time," Abby's dad said gently. "Personally, I don't really care whether or not she plays basketball. As long as she's keeping up with her schoolwork, my only other concerns are that she's safe and that she's enjoying herself. I know it's not right to let your team down, so Sarah will have to talk to the coach if she decides to change her focus. Still, school is all about figuring out what interests you and what doesn't." He paused, and then gazed at Abby intently. "It makes me sad to know that you and Sarah haven't been talking much. Is everything okay between the two of you?"

"Sure, Dad," Abby said grumpily. "No problem here."

"Abby," her mother said gently, "you and Sarah are different people, but Dad and I see you both. Sarah's not the only one we're proud of, you know."

"Yeah, *sure*," Abby retorted.

"Abby, all we want is to see you kids enjoy yourselves," her father told her. "Today I saw you having a great time on the court, and that was terrific to watch. Now I can't wait to see Sarah and hear how her afternoon went. Not everything has to be a competition."

"We support you one hundred percent," her mom agreed. "We just want you to be happy."

Just then, Sarah bolted out the theatre door. She was wearing a dress and tights again, and carrying a thick stack of paper. She raced to the car, pulled open the car door, and hopped inside. Abby watched as her parents turned to look at Sarah expectantly.

"I got it! I'm in charge of props!" Sarah exclaimed. When Abby saw her parents' joyful expressions, she was filled with jealousy.

"Great," she said flatly. She slumped down in her seat, feeling discouraged.

12 PROBLEMS AT PRACTICE

On Tuesday Sarah was waiting by Abby's locker before basketball practice. "I got out of class early so I thought I'd wait for you," she said.

"Oh, you're actually coming to practice? Don't you need to go hang out with the theatre club or something?"

"No, it'll be awhile before I have to start showing up after class. I need to build everything first and I can do that on my own at home," Sarah said.

"Well, I'm glad you're so excited about it," Abby said, grabbing her gym clothes and shutting her locker. "Too bad you aren't as excited about winning the Districts."

"What do you mean? I'm just as excited about playoffs as you are."

"I doubt it," said Abby. "If you really wanted to win, you wouldn't have taken on something else at the same time as basketball. Where's your focus? It was your idea to try out for the team, remember? Obviously you weren't too serious about it." She sped up, forcing Sarah to half-run in order to keep pace with her.

"Abby, lots of people at school are involved with more than one thing. I'm not the only one on the team who's doing something else! Jessie's in the photography club and Emiko writes for the *Harewood Herald*."

"What? Does Coach Marshall know that?" Abby asked, surprised.

"Of course she does! Have you ever heard her say that basketball needs to be our lives, all the time? She has never, ever said that. We don't have to devote every single *moment* of our lives to the Hawks! It's a sport, Abby. Figure it out." Sarah shook her head in exasperation and strode ahead of Abby into the change room.

Abby stood alone in the hallway for several minutes, her mind racing as she stared at the change-room door. She wanted to go in and talk with Sarah but she just couldn't make her feet move.

Sarah's wrong, Abby decided. *She's not taking the team seriously, and she's going to hurt our chances.*

Abby finally pushed open the door and followed her sister inside, but by that time, Sarah was already changed and heading into the gym. With a sigh, Abby set her backpack down, unzipped it, and pulled out her basketball clothes.

"Are you okay, Abby?" Jessie asked.

Abby nodded curtly. "Yeah, thanks Jessie. I just have a lot on my mind."

★★★

"Break into groups of three," Coach instructed as the Junior Hawks gathered in the gym. "Today's all about shooting. Pass-pass-shoot is what I'm looking for."

She grouped Abby, Sarah, and Sam together for the drill. Each time Coach blew her whistle, a new group started across the gym, passing the ball back and forth until the centre took a shot on net.

"When you get back at the end of the line, switch your centre," Coach Marshall reminded them.

Abby, Sam, and Sarah moved to the starting point. The whistle blew and Sam dribbled toward the basket, pivoted, and passed to Sarah. Sarah passed quickly to Abby. As soon as Abby made the jump shot, she knew it was going in. It just felt right.

"Nice one!" Sarah shouted. Abby didn't even look at her.

The three of them took their place at the back of the line, switching off so Sam could play centre, and then Sarah. Sam made her shot, but Sarah's bounced off the rim.

"Wow, you're usually a really good shot," Abby said sweetly. "Is something else on your mind?" A second later she regretted the comment. *Why can't I just leave her alone?* Abby asked herself.

Sam gave Abby a surprised look, and Sarah pretended not to hear. Coach Marshall hadn't heard Abby's comment, but she ran over with some feedback for Sarah.

"It's not all going to be perfect once you're in a tough game," she said. "Nice try, Sarah."

As Abby watched her sister thank the coach, she wondered if the feedback would have been so positive if Sarah had missed that shot in a playoff game.

Next, Coach set everyone up to play keep-away. Abby stood between Sarah and Sam and tried to intercept as they moved the ball back and forth. Sarah eventually fumbled a pass, giving Abby possession.

"Got pirate props on your mind?" Abby needled.

"I'm ignoring you," Sarah said.

"Nice work, Abby," Coach Marshall said. "It's great to see you and Sarah playing together again, by the way."

"Thanks, Coach," Abby said. "Hopefully Sarah manages to make it to a few more of our games." Abby couldn't believe the words that were flying out of her mouth, but she just couldn't stop them.

"Okay, that's *it*," Sarah yelled.

"Will someone tell me what's going on?" Sam demanded. "You two are really annoying to practice with. What's your problem?"

"The problem is Abby," Sarah said. "Apparently no one on the team is allowed to do anything besides school and basketball. I got picked to make props for the school play and now Abby says I'm not *committed* to the team."

Coach Marshall looked surprised. "There's no problem with you making props for the play," she said. "You checked that out with me already. It's completely fine."

"How are we supposed to win back the championship if half the players are focused on other stuff?" Abby challenged the coach. "When Sarah and I tried out for the Junior Hawks, you said we had to stay motivated. You told us we had to win back the championship. Now it seems that you don't care whether or not people are focused on the team."

"You are way out of line, Abby," Coach Marshall said, her expression concerned. "At the start of the year, I said the top priority on our athletics agenda was winning back the championship. I never suggested that players would be punished for having lives outside the team! You owe Sarah an apology. In fact, you owe everyone an apology for disrupting practice."

Abby couldn't believe what she'd just heard. She was sure Coach Marshall had meant that the players had to focus on basketball and only basketball if they wanted to succeed.

"I'm not going to apologize for doing what *you* told me to do," she said defiantly. "I just want the Hawks to keep getting better. If Sarah misses practices for play rehearsals while I'm here putting in the time, then I end up working twice as hard to cover her when we have a game."

"That's not true!" yelled Sarah.

"I'm a better player than you are!" Abby hollered back. "Coach Marshall told me so after our very first practice! She said she was playing you more so you could get better! How are you going to improve if you start skipping practices right before playoffs?" Abby crossed her arms over her chest. "You just don't get it, Sarah."

Abby's words echoed through the gym, and then everything became silent. When Coach Marshall finally spoke, every girl could hear her even though she barely raised her voice above a whisper.

"I'm sorry, Abby, but you're the one who doesn't get it," she said. "We'll never win the championship if we can't work together as a team, and you're mis-understanding what teamwork is about. Go shower and change, please. You're suspended from the Junior Hawks until you can change your attitude."

"What?" Abby gasped.

"You heard me, Abby," Coach Marshall said firmly. "No basketball for you until after Christmas."

"It's only November!" Abby protested.

"If you don't want to be kicked off the team permanently, you'd better start moving, Abby," Coach Marshall warned. "Go get changed. *Now.*"

★★★

Later that evening Abby repeatedly bounced a basketball against the wall at the end of her bed while Sarah sketched out prop ideas at her desk in the opposite corner of the room. Finally, Abby couldn't stand her sister's silence any more.

"I can't believe I'm off the team!" she complained.

"It makes sense to me," Sarah said.

Abby scowled. She hurled the basketball again, and it hit the wall so hard that the vibrations caused some books to fall off the shelf above Sarah's desk.

"Watch it!" Sarah snapped. She got up to retrieve the books and asked her sister, "Why do you think you're the only one who cares about the championship? Everyone wants to try to make it into the playoffs, but you've made things so uncomfortable that it's tough to enjoy a practice lately."

"That's the team's problem." *Thunk, thunk, thunk* went the basketball on the wall at the end of Abby's bed.

"*You* are the one with the problem, Abby! You're treating everyone like garbage, including me, and I'm your own sister! I was excited to be on a team with you and everything, but not any more." Sarah shook her head sadly. "You're completely losing it. We're not in the NBA!"

"Coach Marshall can't stand me now, and I worked so hard to do a good job. This is your fault, Sarah. You picked that fight today!"

"Abby, come on. You know it's not my fault!"

"I hate you!" Abby screamed. "You ruin everything!"

Sarah glared. "I'm not trying to ruin anything," she said. "I'm just doing things that I think are fun. Remember how to have fun?" She turned back to her sketching.

Abby fired the ball at the wall one more time for good measure, but Sarah didn't react. Instead the bedroom door flew open, revealing the girls' mother in striped pajamas and a wide black hairband.

"Abby, *stop that thunking* and get some sleep. Your coach and Principal Baxter want to meet with you, me, and Dad tomorrow, and it would be nice if we could all get some rest beforehand." She closed the door and Abby threw the ball toward it in frustration. It crashed into the door and then dropped.

Abby pulled the covers over her head and listened as the basketball rolled around on the floor for a minute or so. Once it stopped, all she could hear was the persistent scratching of Sarah's sketching pencil.

13 MEETING WITH THE PRINCIPAL

On the short drive to school on Wednesday morning, Abby's parents tried to get her to talk about how she felt.

"How did things get so bad between you and Sarah?" her father asked, turning to look at Abby as her mother drove. "This isn't like either of you. I'm sorry, Abby — I wish we had been more involved with what was going on at school. What do you need us to do to help?"

"It's not your fault," Abby said. "Sarah and I can deal with our own problems."

"Yes, but it's okay to ask for help," her mother said. "Dad and I should have realized this might happen. It can't be easy being sisters at the same high school."

Abby's mother stopped the car at the high school entrance and flicked the turn signal, waiting for a group of students to get through the crosswalk.

"I'm frustrated with you, Abby, but I'm frustrated with myself too," she continued. "High school is a tough time and you needed more support. We wanted to give you and Sarah your space, but I wish we had asked more questions about how things were going."

"*Now* you start talking about support," Abby said. "All I want is to be taken seriously and to do a good job for the team, but everything I do gets taken the wrong way."

"We take you seriously," her father assured her.

Abby sighed and leaned her head against her window as her mother backed into a parking space close to the front doors. As soon as the car stopped Abby got out, shut the door, and jammed her hands firmly into her jacket pockets.

As she walked into the school with her parents, Abby spotted Lisa getting her books out of her locker. Lisa smiled sympathetically and then dashed up the stairs, her silver sneakers flashing in the winter sunlight streaming through the second-floor window. Abby wished that she could go to class too. Instead, she and her parents made a right turn into the school office and sat down in the waiting room.

Abby stared straight ahead at the closed yellow door to Principal Baxter's office. A few minutes later the door opened and Coach Marshall waved them inside.

Abby remembered the principal's office from the fundraising meeting she'd had there with the coach. The violet on the principal's windowsill had five or six more blooms since then. The office had a large window overlooking the playing field, and, next to the violets, a family photo of the principal, her husband, and two young daughters. The principal's hair was a little shorter in the picture, but it was styled in the same way, sprayed and precise like a TV news anchor's. Aside from the fake black leather chairs they were sitting in, the only furniture was a desk and a bookcase with a tropical-looking potted plant sitting on top.

"Thank you all for coming," said Principal Baxter. She smiled warmly and Abby noticed that her teeth were as white and polished-looking as her business shirt.

"Abby, I understand we have a problem to deal with today."

Abby shrugged. "I can't do anything right, I guess."

"Can you tell me why you feel that way?" asked Coach, sliding forward in her seat. She looked at Abby and her parents expectantly. Abby just shrugged again. She had an idea of what she wanted to say but she couldn't make the words come out. After a moment, her dad began to speak.

"When our daughters decided to try out for the Junior Hawks, we thought it was a great idea. I played basketball in high school, and I loved it. Sure, it was about teamwork and discipline, but it was also a lot of fun," Abby's father said. "At home, the girls have had a basketball hoop attached to my workshop wall since they were nine and ten years old. They always enjoy themselves out there, and because of this, they decided to try out for the team."

"Well, no one doubts their commitment to basketball —" began the principal, but Abby's father wasn't finished talking.

"It's been months since the girls shot hoops together at home. They aren't interested in hanging out together at all. This team has driven my daughters apart because Abby is so invested in your need to win back the district championship."

Sure, Dad, tell them it's all my fault, Abby thought angrily.

"To Sarah, basketball is just a fun school sport, but to Abby, it's everything," Abby's mother explained. "She doesn't want to let you down so she tries and tries, at the expense of her happiness *and* her relationship with her sister." She sighed.

"Our daughters have never been competitive. Now they're avoiding each other." She looked at Coach Marshall. "What do you think about all of this?"

"I've definitely noticed that Abby is fired up about winning the Districts," Coach Marshall said. "At tryouts in September, I said that I wanted a team of girls who were prepared to work, but I absolutely did not mean that they had to live and breathe basketball. I stressed the importance of teamwork, fun, and school spirit. The Junior Hawks represent the school to the community, so obviously what we're looking for is a group that can learn from one another and support one another."

"That's not what I remember hearing," Abby said.

"Don't you remember the talk I gave before tryouts?" Coach Marshall asked. "It was all about teamwork, and school spirit, and helping one another to learn."

"I must have missed that part," Abby admitted. "I really don't remember any of that stuff."

Her mother smiled. "I think Sarah does," she said. "Do you remember that conversation we had at the supper table, after the first game the Junior Hawks lost?"

"Maybe," Abby said, but she remembered all too well. *I thought Sarah was just trying to make me look bad when she said all that stuff about teamwork and fun and representing Harewood Secondary in the community*, she thought.

Coach leaned forward. "It would help us all, Abby, if you could tell us why you think this has happened. I'm not sure I understand why you are so competitive with Sarah, and so negative about her work with the theatre club."

"Basketball is something I can do well. I feel like I'm better at basketball than Sarah is, and I don't feel that way about very many things. She's so good at everything." Abby looked up at her mother, who nodded, her expression serious.

"She makes friends, she makes props, and she made the basketball team even though she doesn't take it as seriously as I do," Abby said. "Now she gets to play basketball *and* get involved with theatre, and she'll do well at both." She took a deep breath and then continued. "Instead of getting compliments like Sarah always does, I just get in trouble while everyone keeps telling Sarah how great she is."

Abby looked up and saw understanding in her father's eyes.

"Abby, we are so proud of everything you do," he said softly. "You're every bit as talented as Sarah, and you do a great job of everything you take on." He paused, and then added, "Sarah's your biggest fan, you know."

Abby frowned and looked away.

"I agree with your dad," said Coach Marshall. "Do you remember when I told you that you're a stronger player than Sarah is? You joined this team as one of its strongest players. All you had to do was keep up the effort and develop your skill at our practices. You didn't need to go to any extremes to get noticed. I always noticed you."

Abby nodded. *Don't start crying,* she told herself. She didn't respond and for several seconds the room was completely quiet.

"So what happens now?" asked Abby's mother.

"Abby is still suspended," said Coach Marshall. "I can't have players showing disrespect to each other." She turned to the principal. "We'll stick with our original plan — I'm happy to let her start practicing again in January."

Principal Baxter smiled at Abby. "Does that work for you?"

"I guess," said Abby.

The principal turned to Abby's parents. "Sometimes it's hard for us as educators to get a full idea of a student's motivation," she said. "Thank you for helping us work through this."

As her parents shook hands with Principal Baxter and Coach Marshall, Abby thought about Sarah. *She has no idea how I feel*, Abby thought glumly. *The harder I try, the more miserable I am . . . and the more trouble I get into.*

14 ALL IN GOOD TIME

On Saturday when Abby woke up, the glowing green numbers on her alarm clock read 7:15. Abby peeked over at Sarah's side of the room and noticed that her sister wasn't in her bed. *She probably fell asleep in front of the TV*, Abby thought. She forced herself out from under her covers, threw on some sweats and a hoodie, and grabbed the basketball. She needed to keep practicing, or she'd be out of shape and awkward when her suspension was over.

An hour later, Abby was still at it. She was making most of her shots, but her goal for the morning was to sink ten in a row and she couldn't seem to get past seven. She was about to start another round when the door to her father's shop opened and Sarah stepped out.

"Whoa, sorry!" said Abby. "I didn't know you were in there. I thought you were asleep in the den or something."

"That's okay, you weren't bugging me," Sarah said. "I was just doing some sanding. It was nice to know somebody else was awake."

"What are you making? Props? Can I see?"

Sarah hesitated and then shrugged. "Sure, why not?" She pushed the workshop door all the way open and gestured for Abby to follow her inside. It took Abby's eyes a minute to adjust to the semi-darkness of the shop. Sarah's project was just past the workbench in the open, central area. Abby gasped.

"Wow!" she said. "You made that?" It was a pirate's treasure chest big enough for a person to crouch inside, with thick rope handles on the sides and a vintage-looking lock on the front.

"Mostly," Sarah said, her voice a bit guarded. "Dad helped a lot with the lid, and it was his idea to use rope for the handles. I found the lock at a thrift store. It's not painted yet, obviously, but I think it looks pretty good so far."

"It looks great," Abby told her sister. "I'm completely impressed."

"I made a plank as well," Sarah said with rising enthusiasm. She pointed just past the treasure chest to a wooden springboard that Abby could imagine some poor soul inching along, as pirates forced him or her to take a plunge into the sea. Abby laughed delightedly.

"Sarah, this is perfect."

"Dad helped with that one too."

"I'm so sorry I messed things up," Abby blurted out. "I was jealous of you . . . you made friends with the whole team almost right away, and you started off playing way more than I did. Then you got to do all of this cool stuff too. I just couldn't handle it. You didn't deserve for me to be so mean." She sighed. "I feel like a huge dork."

"Well, you kind of are." Sarah replied. "Do you think I've never felt jealous of you? You waltz around with your name on the honour roll and your life all organized and perfect. It's totally maddening. I figured something out, though. I'm never going to be as good at those things as you are, so I don't try. I *let it go*. Why can't you just do the same thing?"

"Good point," said Abby softly. "Like I said, I'm a dork."

"Abby, I wanted to try out for the team with you because I thought it sounded like fun, *and* because I wanted to hang out with you at school. I was nervous about trying out for the team and I knew it would be a little less scary if you were there too. It all went wrong, though. It ended up not being much fun playing on a team with you, and now we don't hang out together at all."

"Oh," said Abby. *I didn't know Sarah ever felt nervous about stuff like that*, she thought. "Weren't you nervous about getting involved with the theatre too?" she asked.

"Of course I was! That's why I didn't tell anybody except Mom and Dad." Sarah glanced at Abby shyly. "I didn't tell you because I was scared you'd laugh."

"Why would I laugh?"

"Well, because building props is such a *job*. It's a serious thing and you have to focus and make deadlines and finish things on time . . . you're the one who is good at those things. I tend to get distracted."

Abby smiled warmly. "Well, it doesn't look like you're getting distracted here, Sarah. I think these props are amazing."

"Thanks." Sarah said again, beaming.

Abby hesitated and then asked her sister, "Do you want to play a little one-on-one?"

Sarah looked uncomfortable. "Thanks for asking, but I'd rather keep working on this."

"Oh, okay." Abby tried not to let her disappointment show.

Sarah turned back to the workbench, and Abby let herself out of the shed and picked up the basketball again.

15 ANOTHER CHANCE FOR ABBY

When report cards came out just before winter holidays, Abby had top marks except for gym class, where she rated average. *Typical, she thought. I've let a sport take over my life but I still can't ace gym class.* She folded her report, stuck it into her backpack, and hurried down the hall for her lunchtime meeting with Coach Marshall.

"Come on in, Abby," Coach said kindly, and closed her office door to dull the constant noise coming from the hallway. She didn't have a meeting table, but she invited Abby to spread her lunch out on a corner of her desk, and then faced Abby across the narrow space, periodically taking bites from a chicken salad sandwich.

"Good work on your grades, Abby," she said kindly. "You've really done well, and I've noticed you and Sarah are friendlier toward each other these days. How are things between the two of you at home?"

She still isn't interested in spending much time with me, Abby thought.

"Sarah is really busy, but we're getting along when

we do see each other," she replied, trying not to sound glum.

"That's good," Coach Marshall said approvingly. "Do you feel ready to start practicing with the Hawks again in January?"

"Yes, please!" Abby said eagerly.

"Excellent," Coach Marshall said. "Just remember, the Districts are important, but your relationship with Sarah is far more important than any championship — or any team, for that matter."

"I know," Abby said.

Coach Marshall smiled. "I'm glad to hear it," she said. "Now, we have one more thing to discuss. You did a great job with the car-wash fundraiser and we only have a bit of money left to raise. The problem is, I am not allowed to let you do any organizing while you're suspended from the team." She leaned forward and made eye contact with Abby. "How would you feel if I asked Sarah to organize the next fundraiser? The reason I ask is that if your sister chooses to let you help her out with the planning part, there's no way the school can really monitor that."

"So . . . what you're saying is that you'd like Sarah and me to organize something together?" Abby started to feel protective of her fundraising job, and then caught herself. Sarah didn't care about outshining Abby. If she chose to help, she'd be doing Abby a favour.

"If you like," Coach Marshall said warily.

Abby smiled broadly. "Yes, you can ask Sarah to organize a fundraiser while I'm suspended."

"Excellent," Coach Marshall replied.

***

Coach Marshall told Sarah about the idea at practice that afternoon, and that night as they were getting ready for bed, Sarah came over to Abby's side of the room and perched on the edge of her desk.

"I said I'd organize the final fundraiser for the Hawks," she said cautiously. "I hope that's okay with you."

"I was hoping you'd say yes!" Abby said happily.

"If I agree to work with you, can you please just drop the attitude you've had toward me?" Sarah asked. "I want to help the Hawks, and I want to help you. I don't care if this fundraiser makes more or less money than the one you planned, and I don't care whether the other girls think I'm cool for doing the job or whatever. I just want to get along, do the work, and move on. Is that all right with you?"

"It is," Abby promised.

"Okay," said Sarah. "We'd better get busy, then. What do you think about having a pancake breakfast before school one morning?"

"That's a great idea," Abby said. "We could have a choice of pancakes, a choice of juice, and tons of syrup.

We could charge three dollars a plate."

"Perfect," agreed Sarah. "Pancakes are cheap to make, so we'd be able to raise the rest of the money really easily!" She left the room, and a minute later, Abby heard her running down the stairs. Soon Sarah returned with an all-day-breakfast cookbook that belonged to their parents. "I think this is the one with all the cool ideas for crazy pancake and waffle toppings," she said. "Didn't you make a big family breakfast out of this cookbook one time?" She sat down on the bedroom floor and opened up the book. Abby knelt down beside her sister and leaned over her shoulder, excited to help.

16 SUCCESS!

Abby's first day back on the team was the same day as the pancake breakfast. Armed with six huge bottles of maple syrup, Abby, Sarah, and Lisa caught a ride to school with Lisa's dad just after six in the morning. Coach Marshall was already there, measuring out manageable bowls of pancake mix from an industrial-sized paper bag. Several more bags of mix lined the kitchen counter.

"Oh good, you brought the extra syrup," she said. "You can stick it in the fridge with the butter and the syrups I brought."

"Sounds good," Abby said. "Thanks again for being here to help us out."

"No problem," Coach said. "I love pancakes — and besides, the school wanted at least one staff person to keep an eye on things. How could I say no?" She smiled at Abby. "Welcome back!"

The four of them got to work setting up tables with napkins, cutlery, syrup, and butter, and as teammates arrived, they pitched in to help.

By seven-thirty the cafeteria was packed. "It seems as if the whole school is here," Sarah said. She was pouring orange juice into cups that were snatched up as rapidly as she placed them on the counter.

"You might be right," Abby agreed. "I think I've handed over a couple hundred plates of pancakes already." She leaned over the counter and called out to Lisa, Sam, and Jessie, who were working the door. "What's the count so far?"

"Two hundred and two, not counting volunteers," Lisa shouted back. Abby was stunned. There were only 326 students at the school — so nearly two-thirds of them had supported the Junior Hawks breakfast. The team had enough for their supplies and their uniforms with some cash left over! Sarah's fundraiser was a huge success.

It feels good to see everyone supporting our team, she thought. She had kept her promise to Sarah and curbed her competitive thoughts — even when some of the girls on the team had been cold to Abby while praising Sarah for all of her hard work. Even that morning, she'd noticed a few of the girls chose not to work with her — even though Sarah had clearly forgiven Abby.

I still need to prove myself to a lot of the girls, Abby reasoned. *I wish they could understand how hard I tried to be a good team player.*

"May I have your attention, please!" Coach Marshall

called out. She was standing in the centre of the cafeteria, surrounded by tables full of students and staff. "It is my pleasure to announce that thanks to all of you and your ravenous hunger, the Junior Hawks basketball team has achieved its fundraising goal. Thank you very much for helping us to pay for our brand-new team uniforms!"

The cafeteria roared with applause. Abby felt proud. *No one has to know that I wish I'd organized this all by myself,* she decided. She thought about what Sarah had said to her while they were talking in their father's shop. Sarah felt overshadowed by Abby sometimes too . . . she just kept her thoughts to herself and didn't make a big deal about it.

If she can do it, I can do it, Abby thought.

"There are two people I'd like to recognize," Coach Marshall continued. "You probably picked up your breakfast from them this morning, but just in case you don't know them, I'm going to ask our fundraising coordinators to step forward. Abby, Sarah, come on out here."

Grinning happily, Abby walked around the counter and out into the room, her arm linked with Sarah's.

"Abby organized the Junior Hawks car wash back in the fall, and Sarah organized today's pancake breakfast," Coach continued. "Not only are they both excellent basketball players, they are also sisters. Please give them a hand."

As their schoolmates applauded, Coach Marshall shook Abby's and Sarah's hands and presented them with a large thank-you card designed to look like a Junior Hawks jersey. Every member of the team had signed the card, and tucked inside was a twenty-dollar gift card for Fresh Ground.

"Sorry we couldn't break the bank on your gift," Coach Marshall joked. "Lisa said you'd enjoy treating yourselves at this coffee shop."

"She was right about that," Sarah confirmed.

"SPEECH! SPEECH! SPEECH!" shouted a boy at a table near Abby. A few others picked up the chant and their voices soon echoed through the cafeteria. Abby glanced at Sarah, who gestured for her to go ahead. Abby stepped forward and the chanting stopped. Everyone watched her expectantly.

"Being a part of this team has made me feel more like a part of this school," Abby said. "Thanks for supporting the Junior Hawks, and thanks to my sister Sarah for planning this awesome breakfast." Everyone clapped again. Sarah waved and shouted her thanks, and the two sisters headed back to the kitchen together.

***

That afternoon, Abby spoke to Emiko and Sam before practice.

"I want you to know I've had a lot of time to think

and I know how badly I let you both down last term," she said. "I just wanted to say sorry."

"Thanks, Abby," said Emiko. "Nobody's perfect, I guess. I'm happy you're back."

"Me too," said Sam. She smiled warmly at Abby and Abby smiled back.

A few minutes later Coach Marshall called a scrimmage and put Abby and Sarah on the same line with Sam. "Just like before," she said, smiling at them. "Let's see how you do."

Marta took her place across from Abby. "Looks like I'm your check," she said, smiling. "I'm glad you're back, but that doesn't mean I'm going to let you beat me. You'll never see the ball if I can help it!"

Abby laughed. "I wish I'd listened to you more," she told Marta.

"You just needed to get used to being part of a team," Marta said. "Now that you're getting better at that, your whole game will probably improve."

Emiko and Sam jumped for the ball and Emiko won easily. She passed to Marta, who passed to Kim before Abby could block her. They ran down the court, with Sarah keeping pace with Kim. When Kim faked a pass to Emiko, Sarah got fooled, but Abby intercepted the ball. She had a clear shot, but Sarah had moved away from Kim and was a lot closer to the net than Abby was.

I can make this shot, thought Abby. *Should I go for it?* She glanced over and saw Sarah watching her.

She's not calling for the ball, Abby realized. *She's positive that I'm not going to pass to her.* Abby knew she needed to show her teammates that she could play well on a line with Sarah. She passed the ball, grinning as she noticed the shocked look on her sister's face. Sarah caught it neatly and put it through the net.

"Excellent teamwork!" Coach Marshall called, and Abby felt as pleased as if she'd sunk the ball herself.

17 THE DECIDING GAME

All through January the Hawks played game after game as teams around the school district struggled to win a place at the championships. Coach Marshall scheduled practices every day — sometimes even twice a day. Their hard work paid off, and once again, they were facing Nanaimo Secondary for a chance at the Districts.

On the day of the game, Sarah and Abby walked to early-morning practice together.

"This is so intense," Sarah said. "I'm either playing basketball or building pirate weaponry. Everything's running together in my mind!"

"*Arrrrr*," Abby replied. "Should we make Nanaimo Secondary walk the plank when they lose, do you think?"

Sarah burst out laughing. "That would be a change from the good-game handshakes at the end!"

"Do you feel ready?"

Sarah took a deep breath and looked directly at Abby. "I have to tell you something," she said.

"Sure."

"Our stage manager is sick and the theatre teacher asked me if I could fill in for opening night."

"Really? That's great! Did you tell Mom and Dad? Are you allowed?"

"Yeah, they're fine with it if I decide it's what I want to do. They said I have to apologize to Coach for backing out of my commitment, but they understand that theatre is what I love." She hesitated. "Here's the thing though . . . the play opens tonight at seven-thirty."

"But we play Nanaimo Secondary at six-thirty! This game is huge!"

"Exactly . . . and opening night is huge too. If there's no stage manager, we'll have to cancel the show. Coach said I have to choose one activity or the other for the rest of the term, and I've decided I'm not choosing basketball." She paused. "I'll tell Coach Marshall today. I'm really sorry, Abby."

Abby stood perfectly still. She took a sip of tea from her travel mug to calm herself down. No more Sarah on the Junior Hawks.

"So this is it, then?" she asked. "You're done with basketball?"

"I think I am, Abby. I love being on the team, but I didn't know how much more fun I was going to have with theatre stuff. I get way more excited about it than I do about basketball."

She took a sip of her own tea, watching her sister's face closely. "Are you mad?"

"No, I guess not," Abby said. "It's just that . . . well, this is *it*, our chance at the Districts." She paused. "I get it, though. You're into this play and you're really good at that stuff, so I guess it makes sense."

"I'm glad you understand," Sarah said. "You're actually the main reason I've stayed on the team this long. Even when you were being a jerk, I really did want to play with you. Even when I was mad at you, I secretly couldn't wait for your suspension to be over." She frowned. "Do you think Sam and Emiko will be mad?"

"Naahhh. Go ahead and bail. They'll manage . . . they'll just call you all kinds of nasty names behind your back."

Sarah looked shocked for a moment and then realized Abby was joking. "Not funny!" she retorted, and put Abby in a mock headlock. The two sisters staggered around the school lawn, laughing and splashing lukewarm tea on each other. Abby shrieked, tossed her travel mug aside, and grabbed Sarah around the waist, trying to put her off balance. They wrestled around on the grass for a few seconds more, and then Sarah let go. Abby stood up, giggling, and redid her ponytail.

"Well," she said once she'd caught her breath, "I guess it's settled then."

★★★

As she warmed up for the game that evening, Abby felt

sad. *It's going to be so weird not playing on a team with Sarah any more*, she thought. At the same time, she knew that Sarah needed to stick with theatre if she enjoyed it so much.

Coach had said the same thing when Sarah told her about her decision to stage-manage the play.

"Part of being a coach is recognizing what's best for your players," she'd told Sarah. "You've told me that basketball isn't what makes you the happiest. The best thing you can do for yourself — and for your team-mates — is to choose the activity that makes you feel happy."

Abby and Sarah had both thought Coach Marshall's words made sense.

Abby jiggled her right leg up and down nervous-ly, waiting for the start. Some players were assembling on the benches and others were milling about on the court. Abby was on the starting line, and she was feeling nervous. *I have to focus on teamwork. I can't make mistakes tonight, no matter how frustrated I get*, she told herself.

"Hi, Abby." Sarah slid onto the bench next to her sister.

"Hey!" said Abby, surprised to see her sister. "I didn't think you'd be here. Aren't you supposed to be over at the theatre?"

"I'm only here for a little while. I'm going to watch the first five minutes and then Dad and I are heading back there," Sarah said. "Mom and Lisa are staying here to watch you."

Abby hugged Sarah. "I wish I could see your opening night, but I think Coach would be sort of mad."

"Don't worry about that, there'll be lots of chances to see it," Sarah said. "Just think about the game. I want to come and see you play in the Districts — and the Provincials!"

"You will," smiled Abby. "Have fun tonight. I know you'll do well." Abby waved as Sarah headed toward her viewing spot near the gymnasium doors.

Right at the tipoff, Abby had a feeling that the Hawks were in a tough spot. The Nanaimo team had a lot of energy and a lot of attitude — they knew they'd be eliminated from the playoffs if they lost to the Hawks.

"You play like a kindergartner," Abby's check sneered as she dug for the ball. Abby spun the ball between her legs and then around her back, working to keep possession. She was eager to shoot and teach her check a lesson, but she remembered Coach's words during the Hawks' matchup against Central.

Anyone can hog the ball and run around on the court with it, Coach Marshall had said. *It takes teamwork to succeed. All you did out there was mess up your teammates and show Central our weaknesses as a squad.*

Instead of shooting, Abby pivoted, searching for an opening. Finally she bounced the ball over to Marta, who connected with Sam. When Sam scored, Abby sighed with relief. Two-nothing for the Hawks.

"You won't be so lucky next time," Abby's opponent

said. The girl's short brown hair was already wet with sweat. When she ran a hand through it, it stood up in spikes like tiny exclamation points. Abby ignored her, but the girl just wouldn't stop yapping.

Marta traded off with Jessie, who almost immediately got the ball to Abby. Her check got the better of her, though, and Nanaimo got a basket. Tie game. The basket seemed to energize the Nanaimo team. Before Abby and her linemates knew it, Nanaimo had managed to score three more times.

"You know you'll never beat us," Abby's check sneered. "We're the District champions and that's the way it's going to stay."

She is so annoying, thought Abby. *I can't let her get to me.* She felt fiercely competitive. She quickly realized that in this situation, however, it was perfectly okay.

Her check got the ball and began to move it forward. Abby watched her check's moves closely. She could see that the girl was getting tired. *Come on . . . give me an opening*, Abby thought. Just then her check stumbled a bit while dribbling, and took her eyes off the ball just long enough for Abby to steal it.

Abby ran down the court with her check close behind. She could see that Jessie had a good chance at scoring, so she passed. Jessie's check fouled her and the shot bounced off the rim. The ref blew the whistle and Jessie took a free throw. She sunk it!

As Abby high-fived Jessie, she thought back to what

Sarah had told her back in the fall —*The team still gets the points if you let someone else sink the basket, you know.*

Abby smiled. She wished she'd spent more time listening to Sarah and less time trying to out-do her on the court.

The next time she got the ball, Abby twisted and turned aggressively, keeping it as far away from her check as she could.

"Give me that!" the girl grunted. She stepped toward Abby as Abby tried to pivot away. The other girl hooked her foot between Abby's feet and both girls went down. The ball shot away across the court.

"Foul!" called the ref. Several players from both teams ran over to help the two girls off the floor.

"Are you okay to play?" Sam asked Abby.

"I'm fine," Abby told her. She stood up and examined a small scrape on her left elbow. The ref motioned for Abby to throw the ball back into play. Abby knew the foul had been intentional but she decided it didn't matter as long as the Hawks still had possession. If she retaliated, she could get thrown out of the game. She threw the ball to Sam and jogged back onto the court, looking for an opening.

Jessie got the ball and passed to Abby.

"Go long!" Jessie shouted.

Abby hesitated. Long shots were Sarah's specialty, not Abby's.

I can make all the same shots as Sarah can, she told

herself. She released the ball and hoped. It whooshed easily through the net.

Abby grinned widely and headed down the court again.

★★★

At halftime, Coach Marshall congratulated the team. "You're doing great out there!" she said. "We're down a few points, but 30–22 isn't bad. We can make it up. Keep the pressure on, though, whatever you do. This team specializes in building a lead late in the fourth quarter."

"Ugh," Sam said. "That's how they stole the championship from us last spring."

"It's not happening again," Emiko said firmly.

By the end of the third quarter, the Hawks had brought the score to 40–34, and Abby's check was even more aggressive.

"You're tired," she told Abby. "I can tell. Every time you get the ball, I'll be there to take it away."

Abby took a deep breath and concentrated on the play. Emiko faked a shot and passed to Abby. Suddenly, her check charged into her and knocked her down, but Abby still managed a pass to Marta.

"That was on purpose — again!" Abby yelled at her check. The ref hadn't noticed, though. There was nothing to do but keep playing. Abby struggled up. Her check was long gone and Coach waved Abby off the court for a break.

"Keep your cool out there, Abby. Don't let it get to you," said Coach, clapping her hand down on Abby's shoulder. "You're doing great." Abby nodded. She drank from her water bottle and then took some deep breaths to calm herself down. She glanced up at the scoreboard — 44–38. The Hawks still had some work to do.

When Coach sent her back onto the court, Abby knew she had to take every opportunity she could to help the Hawks advance. The very next time she got the ball, though, her check tripped her. This time the ref blew the whistle.

"What was that all about?" Emiko asked Abby's check. The girl shrugged, not even looking at Emiko, her gaze a steady challenge as she sized Abby up. Abby looked back at the girl calmly. *She's losing it,* Abby realized. *She's so focused on getting to me that she's hurting her team.*

Play continued and the Hawks closed the gap in the score. Abby passed to Jessie, who scored to make it 48–46. About thirty seconds later, Abby got a chance of her own — a wide-open chance at a three-point shot. It went in!

"Oh yeah?" Abby heard her check growl. The next thing she knew, the girl shoved her with both hands, knocking her to the floor.

"Hey!" Coach screamed from the bench. Abby

pushed herself up to see her linemates running to her side.

She glanced over at the ref, who was talking to both coaches, Sam, and Nanaimo's captain. The ref walked over to talk to Abby's check. A moment later the girl scowled. She ran over to the bench and pulled on her hoodie with a quick, jerky motion.

Abby's check was out of the game!

I got rid of her by staying calm, Abby thought proudly. *A month ago I was so stressed out and worried about points that I might have acted exactly like that girl.*

After Abby's check was ejected from the game, Nanaimo completely lost steam. As the clock ticked down, the Harewood fans all stood up and started stomping and clapping. Emiko sunk a shot, and cheering echoed through the gym.

I can't believe how loud it is in here, Abby thought. The score was 53–48 for the Hawks, then Emiko put the ball through the net one last time to bring the Hawks up to 55.

Abby couldn't even hear the buzzer at the end of the game — she only knew it was over when the players on the Harewood bench raced out onto the court. A lot of the fans ran onto the court too. Abby heard Lisa calling her name and turned toward the sound just as Lisa caught her in a bear hug.

"Abby, you were awesome!" Lisa shouted, grabbing Abby's shoulders and jumping up and down. "You got rid of that nasty girl without getting kicked out of the game, too. Good stuff!"

"Lisa's right," Abby's mom agreed, coming up to join them and patting her daughter on the back. "You did great! That girl was way out of line. I was ready to run out and haul her off the court myself!"

Abby groaned. "I'm glad you didn't, Mom . . . that would have been a bit much. She got what was coming to her." She smiled, and then threw one arm around Lisa and the other around her mom.

"We did it!" Abby exclaimed. "The Hawks are going to Districts!"

18 TEAMWORK

Out by their father's shop the next morning, Abby and Sarah played a little one-on-one while their parents sipped coffee and watched.

"Aren't you girls freezing?" their mother called, zipping up her thermal vest and shaking her head at her daughters' court shorts and light hoodies.

"I'm sweating like crazy!" Sarah called back. "It's not easy keeping up with last night's superstar!"

Abby laughed and slipped past her sister, using an opening in Sarah's defensive play to her advantage. "Come on, Sarah," she teased. "*Fight* me for it!" She made the basket.

Not to be outdone, Sarah lunged for the rebound and put another one in the net. Their father clapped.

"It's great to see you playing together," he said. "I hope you keep it up."

Sarah flopped down next to him. "I'll always play pickup with *Abby*," she said. "I just don't want to be on a *team* any more."

"Well, you are still on a team, in a way," Abby said, bouncing the ball. "You're working with a whole group of people to produce a play."

"I guess that's true," Sarah said. "I definitely feel that way after last night. There's so much to remember and so many things going on at once. I really liked the rush of it."

"I'm proud of you both," their mother said. "The Hawks won against Nanaimo, Abby had a personal best for points, Sarah tried something new and was successful . . . and the best thing is, I know you both really enjoy what you're doing. It's wonderful for me to see my children doing what they love. You've made me a happy mom."

"Don't start crying," their father stage-whispered. "They're *teenagers*. They'll get *embarrassed*."

Abby laughed. "Thanks, Dad, she said. "That was about to get awkward." She hugged her mother tightly. "Thanks," she murmured.

"Yeah, thanks Mom," Sarah said. She turned to her father and asked, "Would you mind helping me fix up the treasure chest and gangplank? Some of the pirates got a bit carried away last night. The props took a beating."

Sarah and their dad headed into the shop, and their mom went to refill her cup with coffee. Abby picked up the basketball again, backing up to her imagined free-throw line. It was going to be a great few weeks — the

Junior Hawks would play in the Districts, and even the provincial junior championship was well within reach.

Abby bounced the ball a few times and then took her shot. As she netted a perfect three-pointer, she imagined it was the final minute of the championship game and her parents, sister, and Lisa were cheering her on.